Night of
No Moon

by

MARGARET CHAPMAN

Harlequin Books

TORONTO • LONDON • NEW YORK • AMSTERDAM • SYDNEY

Original hardcover edition published in 1977
by Mills & Boon Limited

ISBN 0-373-02157-7

Harlequin edition published April 1978

PRINTED IN U.S.A.

CHAPTER ONE

WHERE was he? Why didn't he come?

With a start Faith turned to the Malay who had glided soundlessly up to her.

'No much nice girl come here! I take you home for two dollars?'

The slim, matt-skinned Malay stood by his three-wheeled, man-powered taxi, eyeing Faith hopefully. Respectable girls did not ride in such vehicles, she thought as she hastily gave him a dollar to get rid of him, then she anxiously turned to the river again. He was right, of course; the Singapore waterfront was not the place for a girl at night. And the Chinese section, with its squalid huddle of sampans on the river and its noisy muddle of streets on the shore, was definitely not the place for a girl at night. But Faith knew Singapore dock, she had worked in one of the shipping offices for more than two years and all the sounds and smells, even the dangers were familiar.

Luke would not keep her waiting. Luke was a gentleman! Faith glanced at the river again and then up at the night sky which was already painted by the city's glittering lights, and then down again to where the dark, silver-threaded water lapped lazily at the crumbling, grey wharf stairs. The *tongkangs*, the motorised lighters that carried rice and Malaysian rubber to the ocean-going vessels anchored in the roads, were moored for the night. The air was full of sounds. Malays and Chinese called to each other in low voices, there was the roar of the traffic up in the city and the ringing of an ice-cream vendor's bell. There was the sound of music too, a gentle, strange and soulful music, carried downstream by the west wind from Sumatra. Music full of a melancholy longing, music that mingled uncannily with the full-blooded blasts of Western pop.

Faith moved restlessly again. She was not afraid, but she was uneasy. She had to see Luke Webb. It was imperative that she did so. Luke was the only person who could help her.

And she needed help badly. Jeremy, the man who loved her and whom she loved in return, had vanished without a word. Faith's delicate face twisted with grief. If only he had told her where he was going! To have gone without a word was what she found so agonizing, so shattering, so terrifying. She felt sure that Jeremy was in some terrible trouble. And he did not want to implicate her in any way, she was sure of that too. To disappear had been his way of safeguarding her. But she would not desert him; she loved him and she would prove her love.

But she had to find him first—that was why she had accepted Luke Webb's invitation to a party on board the *English Rose*. Jeremy, an engineer on a tanker named the *Southern Cross*, had often talked of his friends on the *Rose*. He had sometimes gone along to the Sailing Club to have a drink with one or two of the *Rose*'s officers. There was, therefore, just a chance that one of the men would know something; that was why she had got in touch with Luke. She had met Luke Webb in the shipping office. That was how they had become friends. Luke had taken her to a show once or twice. He had also taken her friend. Luke liked a good time; he was not the type to get himself really involved with any girl. But where was he? Why didn't he come?

It was not like him to be late. Faith began to pace up and down the cobbled stones again. As she paced she turned everything over in her mind again. She remembered how Jeremy had complained about the Chinese crew, especially about his number one man, and again her heart contracted with fear. The Chinese crew were always getting into trouble over drugs, Jeremy had often told her so. Faith fought to keep calm.

She thought of Jeremy. Six months ago her parents had been killed in an air crash and if it had not been for her meeting with Jeremy Caithness she felt she would have also died, of grief. He had lifted her out of her misery, her excruciating loneliness. They had fallen in love almost at once. Soon everything was arranged for their marriage and return to England where Jeremy promised to make her a home in an English village. But now she was alone again, alone apart from the girl with whom she shared the bungalow.

A sound made Faith spin round ... and there was

Luke, the First Mate of the *English Rose*. Immaculate and attractive in a dark, lean way, he stepped around a mountain of empty skips, calling as he came, 'Hello, baby! Sorry I'm so late. I bumped into a chap from my last ship and we had a quick drink together.'

Faith gave him a quick smile of relief and thought how dashing he looked in his white tropical kit. 'I should have met you up in the town,' she said with a forced laugh. 'I must say I was beginning to get a little nervous.'

Luke Webb cast a quick, appraising glance over her slim figure, her bronzed limbs and shining tawny hair. 'You look great,' he said and he grinned happily. 'I love your dress. That halter neck suits you.' He grinned again. 'But what about those cork soles? Are they safe?'

'They're very comfortable,' Faith told him as he slipped his arm about her waist and steered her by some packing cases.

'I'd marry you,' he said with an assumed soberness, 'but I couldn't bear to keep leaving you.'

'Thanks for the offer anyhow.' Faith tried to sound lighthearted, but her voice was sober enough when she asked, 'How are we going to get across?'

'Old Ling's taking us,' he told her. 'He's waiting further up the quay.'

'Whose party is it?' Faith asked as they picked their way over the moonlit cobbles.

'The old man's ashore for the night. That's why we're celebrating.'

'The old man?'

'The Captain, sweetie.' Luke gripped her arm. 'Here's Teo Ling,' he said. 'He's prompt enough.' He called out a cheerful greeting and a middle-aged Chinese in drill trousers and indigo blue sweat-shirt came rolling towards them grinning happily.

'No visitor come here,' Teo Ling said the moment his bright eyes met Faith's. 'Have good time. Yes?'

'Of course we're going to have a good time.' Luke's tone was cheerful. 'So let's get started.'

'Engine ready, boss.'

'Good man!' Luke gave the Chinese a friendly enough wink.

Carefully, Faith walked the plank provided and with Luke's aid she jumped down into the *tongkang*. 'That's fine,' she gasped as she landed safely.

But Luke was already squinting up at the sky. 'You'd better get under the shelter,' he told her. 'There could be a squall.'

'I hope not,' Faith returned sharply, smoothing down her white tricel dress and glancing at the clouds overhead. 'The squalls from the west can be quite nasty.' She made her way to the makeshift shelter of arched, corrugated tin and sat down on the edge of the rough seat. 'Never mind,' she called, 'I'm sure your Mr Ling knows what he's doing.'

'Did you ever meet a Chinese who didn't?' Luke laughed, and he bent down to squeeze Faith's hand encouragingly. 'Old Ling has been a lighterman on the river for twenty years,' he told her as he considered her small, anxious face. 'That's a little longer than you've been on this planet, Faith. So relax.'

'I'm all right.' She gave him a quick smile.

But the tone of her voice made Luke pause and frown at her again. 'Are you sure?' he asked, squinting down at her with real concern in his eyes now. 'You seem unusually nervy, Faith. Sure you want to go to the party?'

'Of course!' Faith swallowed hard and then tried to look eager. 'I'm not the girl to miss a party—you know that.' She forced a laugh and glanced to the other end of the small boat. 'It's that engine,' she said. 'It's making me nervous. It sounds rather odd, don't you think?'

Luke frowned and got to his feet. 'Perhaps I'd better take a look at her,' he said. But at that moment the engine ripped into life and they were on their way. Luke returned to Faith with a grin on his face. 'There, what did I say?' he laughed. 'Old Ling knows what's he's doing.'

'All the same,' Faith said in a small voice and as she clung to the crossbar seat, 'I'd be pleased if you'd stay with him, Luke. I'd feel much safer.'

Luke disappeared, and alone beneath her bleak shelter Faith wondered if she would ever feel safe again. Poor Luke, she thought, he was so good. But he knew nothing of her torment. As yet she had not confided in him. She stared out across the dark water and panic filled her again. Where was Jeremy? A stranger six months ago, now no one mattered more than he did. From their first meeting they had been madly in love. She remembered that first time when he had come into the shipping office. She had gone to the counter and their eyes had met and held in enchantment. After that their love affair had been like an obsession. Jeremy had said she was as lovely as any lotus flower, that from the first moment he had ached to take her in his arms. Jeremy, blond, blue-eyed and bronzed—and now he was gone. Only his image was intact in her mind, his last fond caress, his last warm kiss. No one could take those memories from her.

The sound of Luke shouting above the rising wind roused Faith. 'Good man, Ling. That didn't take long.'

'Thank you, boss.' Teo Ling's face seemed to crack into a million pieces. 'Yes, Teo Ling keep you safe.'

Faith felt reassured. There was nothing going on in Singapore harbour that Ling didn't know about. She stared at him again and thought how strange it was the way a Chinese's eyes could say everything and yet nothing.

She turned to the ships and cruisers lit with strings of white electric bulbs and Luke was saying to her, 'There's the *English Rose*, Faith. She's the one that's floodlit and all decked with lights. Just listen to that music! Come along, let me help you on to the gangway.'

The night air rang with voices and within moments a cheerful masculine voice was calling, 'Give me your hand, lady. Welcome to the party!'

A strong arm assisted Faith and then they were on their way to the brightly lit afterdeck where the party was in full swing. Groups of attractively dressed young women and dashing-looking officers all in white dress uniforms were drinking and dancing under the canvas awning. Faith caught her breath. The girls looked like exotic fireflies. Everyone seemed to be enjoying themselves. Pop music blared relentlessly from a loudspeaker.

Luke threw up his arms in a gesture of wild delight as a lithe-hipped girl in a shocking pink sari, with a sprig of jasmine in her sleek black hair, rushed happily over to him. Her eyes glittered as she whispered something against his cheek and with a laugh he cast her hastily away again.

'That was Désirée Greco,' Luke explained. 'And believe me, her mother made no mistake at her christening! She's with the Second Mate. And he's welcome . . .'

Faith had to laugh. She said as she watched Désirée flutter away, 'I didn't expect to see quite so many people, Luke. How did they all get here?'

'By launch, darling. They came earlier.' He slid his arm about her and steered her on to the cleared deck. 'Let's dance,' he said and his grip tightened about her. 'I feel just great.'

For a while they swayed and rocked across the afterdeck and then quite suddenly Luke stopped. 'You're certainly not in a dancing mood,' he said in a disappointed tone and frowning a little as he gazed into Faith's grey-blue eyes. 'You feel like a ton of bricks. What's wrong, Faith? I know there's something . . . There must be.'

'It's a bit too warm,' she said quickly, and drawing him to her so that he could not see the despair in her eyes. And then she forgot Luke and her heart began to beat fast as she realised that someone was eyeing her furtively from the darkened well-deck. She caught her breath and stared over his shoulder, a great explosion of fear in her ears. Instinctively she moved even closer to Luke.

'That's better,' he breathed against her smooth cheek. 'Stay where you are, Faith, and just keep up the motion. Hmm, that's sweet.'

For a moment his lips rested upon her cheek, but she was unaware of it. The beam from one of the swinging lanterns had caught the man's face. It was the face of a Chinese whom she recognised. Their eyes met and held and Faith began to tremble. The Chinese's cold stare was like a dagger at her throat. Yes, she had seen that wrinkled face before. He had been one of the crew on the *Southern Cross*. He was the frightful character whom Jeremy had called Number One.

'What's wrong, Faith? Don't spoil it.' Luke was holding her away from him and frowning again. Then quickly he followed her gaze. He laughed and called to the Chinese in the shadows, 'What are you doing down there? Get back to your work, Tan Chow!'

Without a word, the Chinese steward mounted the steel ladder and slipped away on soundless feet.

Luke watched him go, then he pulled a face and told Faith, 'He can cook, but that's about all. He came to us from the *Southern Cross*, so he's a damned lucky fellow. Most of that crew will be in jail now.'

'In jail?' Faith felt her blood drain away from her and she gripped Luke's arms for support. 'But why?' she whispered.

'Drugs,' Luke said in an undertone, but he did not get time to tell Faith any more, for unexpectedly a gigantic shadow fell across the deck and glancing up, Faith gasped with alarm. She had never before seen such a large man, nor such a striking one. He was over six feet tall, with broad shoulders, large, dark burning eyes with immensely thick black eyebrows over them. His features were strong and sculptured, his cheekbones high, his nose hawk-like. His black hair was tumbled and waved deeply and a fuzz of black hair appeared just over the top button of his white shirt. His face was motionless, his anger controlled.

'My God!' Luke said under his breath. 'It's the old man! He's back.'

'Mr Mate!' A deep, powerful voice sounded through the night air.

Luke, springing to attention at once, answered, 'Yes, sir. We're having a small celebration.'

'I'm not blind, Mr Mate.' The voice held cold sarcasm.

Staring at him, Faith felt herself cringe. This stranger fascinated and terrified her.

'Would you care to join us, sir?' Luke's voice shook slightly.

'You know damned well I wouldn't.' The Captain stepped forward.

He was a giant. But what struck Faith most was the fact that he was not an old man. He could be little more than thirty. She thought he was the most fearless-looking man she had ever seen. As the beam from a lantern caught his face she saw that his eyes were coffee-coloured and that they were focused coldly upon her.

'May I introduce Miss ...' Luke began hesitantly.

'You may not.' The Captain snapped at the air with hard fingers. 'Get the deck cleared, Mr Mate.' Completely ignoring Faith, he went on brusquely, 'And be on the bridge in ten minutes. We're sailing at dawn.'

Luke drew his hand across his brow in a gesture of both alarm and exasperation. 'I'm sorry about that,' he said, making a face at Faith. 'I'm afraid Captain Hilliard is not the most mannerly type.'

Faith was not thinking of the Captain now. She gripped Luke's arm. 'Luke,' she began quickly, 'tell me what happened on the *Southern Cross*. I knew one of the engineers ...'

'He's probably in jail too, then,' Luke said as he anxiously brushed her off. 'The crew had just about everyone involved.'

'In jail?'

'Either that or he's made a break for it. I did hear

that some of them managed to get away. He's probably on another ship by now.'

'I see.' Faith was shivering again and she crossed her arms about herself. 'You'd better go,' she said. 'Your Captain even has me scared.'

'He's all right,' Luke laughed. 'In fact where the men are concerned, he's fair enough. Hilliard's a man's man. He likes his whisky and his books, and his music. But for him, women are out. Obviously they don't bother him.'

'Perhaps they bother him too much,' Faith laughed, thinking of the giant with the coffee-brown eyes.

'Not Captain Hilliard,' Luke pressed. 'He's self-sufficient. He knows what he wants and he makes sure he gets it.'

'You'd better get to the bridge, then, Luke.'

'Stay here, Faith,' Luke told her swiftly. 'Don't move. Teo Ling should be around somewhere. I told him to wait.'

Faith nodded, watched Luke disperse the dancers and then turned to gaze out across the South China Sea. Her tawny head drooped. What had happened? Had Jeremy sailed away somewhere? No man in his right senses would want to be involved with the smuggling of drugs. For a few moments she fought back her tears, her sensitive mouth quivered in prayer. If the worst had happened, then she hoped with all her heart that Jeremy had got away. When all was well he would get in touch with her again— their love was big enough to stretch out across the world. She closed her eyes. She was so lonely.

Suddenly she moved back in terror as a hand reached out and touched her arm. She whirled round. It was the Chinese steward, Tan Chow, again. She stared at him in terror while his old parchment face cracked into a maze of wrinkles. He had a parcel and he thrust it upon her.

'Present,' he gabbled in broken English. 'Nice present for missy.' His slit eyes grew longer, the smile disintegrated. 'Miss make no trouble for Tan Chow?'

Trembling, Faith stared back at the Chinese. She was right, she had seen him before. And he recognised her. As though she held a bomb she thrust it back at him. 'I don't want your bribe,' she gasped. 'I want to know where the Second Engineer of the *Southern Cross* has gone. I must know. If you'll tell me I'll not speak out.' Taking a chance, she lowered her voice and told him, 'I know you're involved.'

Her bluff worked. For ten seconds the Chinese stared back at her with eyes bright with murderous hostility. Then the smile was back on his face and after a furtive glance over his shoulder, he told her quickly, 'Engineer gone to Bali—truth. Second Engineer gone to Bali.'

'Bali? The island?'

'Yes, Missy. Missy no make trouble?'

Breathless with emotion, Faith nodded. 'Me no make trouble,' she repeated, and Tan Chow vanished into the darkness.

Faith turned back to the great dark ocean. So Jeremy had managed to escape. He had managed to get on a ship going to Bali. Her young face creased with emotion. How was she going to get to Bali? She had to find a way.

Luke came back looking agitated and flushed and Faith asked as calmly as she could, 'Well, have you sent everyone home? Have you got your sailing orders?'

'Yes, I have,' Luke answered her. 'We're not wasting any time. We're off to Bali.' He grinned again and his gaze strayed over Faith. 'I love Bali,' he told her more cheerfully. 'I just wish I could take you with me, Faith.'

Faith turned to the sea and smiled at the idea. Then her heart beat faster. Luke, unwittingly, had put an idea into her head. Yes, she would go with the ship to Bali! She would stow away! It was a crazy, mad idea, perhaps even dangerous, but she must not hesitate. She had to do it now. Her love for Jeremy would give her courage and strength.

Soaked to the skin in her hiding place on the dimly lit well-deck, Faith listened to Teo Ling's shrill call from his lighter. 'No wait. Too bad squall. Missy go with launch? Yes!'

Luke's strained voice battled against the wind and lashing rain. 'She must have done,' he shouted. 'All right, you'd better push off.'

But Missy had not gone with launch. Faith smiled and laid her wet cheek against the steel plating of the bulwark and waited with fast beating heart. The lighter's engine ripped into life and she heard Luke bellowing, 'Right, Ling, take her round!'

Peering up through the ship's rails, she saw the lighter's stern light rising and falling in the darkness. Teo Ling was not taking any chances; he was off for the harbour. He knew the Sumatra squall too well.

She moved painfully. She was shaken and frightened, yet wildly exhilarated. The weather had come to her aid and made the decision for her. In the confusion and excitement she had managed to slip away undetected. Only ten minutes or so ago it had been an absurd idea, but now the deed was done. There was no turning back; she had stowed away. She was scared, terrified, shaking from head to foot as she wondered where to hide. Then she remembered that Luke had told her that one of the engineers had left the ship in Singapore. That meant an empty cabin.

Somehow she had to find it.

Glancing up, Faith saw the bridge deck and the lit-up wheelhouse, and the lights along the accommodation alleys. She could see that there were two figures in the wheelhouse. One was Captain Hilliard, the other was Luke. A number of officers had gone back to the mainland with the girls, but she knew that they would be returning very soon.

On her hands and knees, she made her way cautiously along the side of the bulwark until she reached the ladders up to the bridge deck. The steel rungs were slippery, but she managed to clamber up them. Once on deck, with shoulders still bent and head down, she made a run for the first dimly lit accommodation alley. The first two cabins were lit up, so she slipped quietly by them and then, exhausted, fell pantingly against the third door.

With fear in her throat, she reached for the door handle and curled her trembling fingers about it. It was unlocked, and her heart leapt up with hope—but only for a brief moment. A light footfall behind her froze her into immobility. A hand reached out from the shadows and twig-like fingers scratched over her bare shoulder. Faith swayed, closed her eyes and waited for the worst.

It was Tan Chow. Faith opened her eyes again as his soft voice purred with assumed solicitude. 'Missy wants to be our guest a little longer?'

She turned quickly, loathing the strange smile on his face. She knew that it would be fatal for her to lose face, to appear afraid. She took a deep breath and stared back defiantly at Tan Chow. 'I must go to Bali,' she said in a lowered but level voice. 'I must find a friend of mine, Jeremy Caithness—he's the Second Engineer on the *Southern Cross*. Tan Chow, you must help me.'

Tan Chow's oblique eyes narrowed until they almost disappeared. 'Caithness take missy to England?'

There was something in his question that shook her. She nodded and backed even harder against the cabin door. She did not trust the Chinese; there was something about his contemptuous leer, his glittery eyes, that terrified her. She felt he knew something that she did not. But what?

'You're sure the engineer Caithness went to Bali?' she breathed.

'Sure. This ship go there too.'

Faith wanted to ask him more, but she saw his expression change suddenly and his bone-thin body stiffen. She felt herself being pushed forward, then the cabin door opened and in a hasty undertone, Tan Chow was saying, 'Quick—in here! Tan Chow help.'

There was no time to hesitate. Faith felt his hard hand, like a fist full of bones, send her scrambling back into the dark cabin and before she could steady herself the door had shut quietly. There was a soft clicking noise and in horror she stared through the darkness. Tan Chow had locked her in! Instinct made her want to cry out in alarm, bang and kick at the door, declare herself. But once again she thought of Jeremy and of their great love for each other and she grew calm. Jeremy was in Bali. She *had* to get there.

She turned in the darkness and tried to get her bearings. The bunks, she knew, would be opposite the door. She took three good steps forward and felt herself hard against a built-in bed. There was only one, and she ran her hand along the hard wooden boards. The bed was not made up, so she was lucky. They intended that the cabin should remain empty. And unlucky too, Faith thought, because she felt so weak and shaken and there was nowhere for her to lie down. She groped about the cabin for a short time and found a wash-basin, and cupping her hands together she managed to get a cool drink. Then she slid down to the floor and sat for a while with her back against the wall, waiting for her eyes to grow accustomed to the darkness.

Soon they did. Now it was not so black; she could even make out the porthole. There was a flimsy curtain drawn across it. Painfully she got up and drew it back. The south-west monsoon was now at work; lightning pulsed in the black clouds. There was nothing else to see, just the great neon-like streaks.

Afraid and lonely, Faith turned back to her small dark prison. Then she fell against something and gave a little cry. After the pain had subsided she did a little investigating and found that she had stumbled upon some sheets of Malaysian rubber. She picked up as many of the sheets as she could and spread them out on the bunk bed.

Lying in her makeshift bed, she thought of Jeremy. To comfort herself she thought of the wonderful days they had spent together. And now she did not even know where Jeremy was. He had gone without a word; he had just disappeared. She had only Tan Chow's word that he was in Bali. He was innocent of any crime, she knew that. Everyone had told her; Jeremy Caithness looked what he was ... a good, clean Englishman. So why had he gone away?

It was four o'clock in the morning when Faith eventually fell asleep, and she was still asleep when the church near the dock rang the Angelus, as Singapore's packed city stirred and the quay started its day-long stream of traffic between wharf and oceangoing ship. Faith finally stirred when, at seven o'clock, the *English Rose* cast her moorings and started out for the deep China Sea.

It was the roar of the ship's engines that made her sit up abruptly. She took a deep tremulous breath, rubbed her eyes—and then she remembered everything.

Fighting to keep calm, she listened intently to the calls and cries that rose above the sound of the engines. Someone was shouting atrociously—she had never heard such curses! She was in a man's world now. She thought of Tan Chow and her skin began to creep, her spine growing icy cold again. Perhaps Tan Chow had some evil plan of his own? What would happen to her if he did not come back to the cabin? She had seen both impudence and contempt in his eyes. What if the Chinese was no friend of Jeremy's? The idea made Faith tremble, then she pulled herself together. If the worst happened she could bang on the door and declare herself.

But she would give Tan Chow a chance. She was on her way to Bali and that was where he had said Jeremy had gone. She climbed down from her high bed and tiptoed to the porthole. Yes, they were on the high seas now; there was to be no turning back. She stared down at her dress and gasped in dismay. It was dirty, torn and crumpled. But she still had her small handbag. The idea made her smile; whatever happened, whatever the catastrophe, a woman held on to her bag. And what luck—there was a mirror above the wash-basin.

Quickly and as silently as possible, she sluiced her face and then patted it dry with the hem of her dress. She ran a comb through her long hair and after that she brightened her lips with a salmon pink lipstick. After she had done her best to look attractive she felt better, more sure of herself. She was confident that Tan Chow would help her and at least bring her something to eat.

But Tan Chow did not come, and after a while Faith got up to get a drink at the wash-basin again. It was a long day of familiar sounds and imagined terrors, and twice she got up for another drink. When the sun was high she got up and searched her handbag thoroughly, but there was nothing, not even a fragment of chocolate. With an impatient angry gesture she flung the bag down, then curled up on one of the Malaysian rubber sheets.

There was a faint tapping sound at the door and a soft voice whispered, 'Tan Chow, missy. Bring food.'

Faith heard the soft click of the key in the lock and then the door opened slowly and she backed away. She did not entirely trust Tan Chow. Even though he was helping her to get to Bali she still did not trust him. But she took the parcel he thrust into her shaking hands and the small flask. 'What time is it, Tan Chow?' she whispered.

'One hour to nightfall, missy.' The Chinese glanced furtively back over his shoulder. 'Must go quick, missy.'

But he was not quick enough and to Faith's horror and dismay the door was suddenly kicked wide open and an angry voice demanded, 'What the devil are you doing in here, Tan Chow?'

Faith, recognising the voice, felt her blood drain away. She shrank back behind the door.

Tan Chow tried to escape, but was being hauled back. Now Faith could hear him babbling in rapid, excited Chinese, then breaking into English, 'Missy give me big scare!'

'Missy!' Captain Hilliard sounded stunned. 'What's going on in here?'

There was nothing she could do now. Limp with shock, Faith hid behind the door and waited to be discovered. Captain Hilliard entered the cabin and was looking round him. His eyes narrowed suspiciously and then he pulled back the door.

Faith saw the anger in his face and for a moment she thought he would strike her. The coffee-brown eyes glared at her from beneath their thick black brows. Then as though shocked himself, the Captain leaned back against the cabin door, closing it with a smart slam. Instinctively Faith began to move away, but his probing gaze followed her.

Weak with fright, Faith watched a pulse working at the side of the Captain's mouth. She knew that he had the wrong idea about her and she wanted to cry out angrily and tell him so, but terror gripped her like a vice and she could only stand and gape back at him.

'What's your name, girl?'

It was the coldest, sternest voice Faith had ever

heard, and while she groped for strength to answer him, he enquired again, 'Your name? I suppose you've got one?' His cold, contemptuous eyes were lowered to her bedraggled dress.

Still Faith could not speak, but her grey eyes entreated, 'I'm not a cheap, silly girl out for kicks. I'm not even permissive. I'm not what you think.'

The Captain had other ideas. He took her arm in a merciless, vice-like grip. 'I don't suppose you have any address either?' His eyes were insolent.

Although terror-stricken, Faith fought to retain her dignity. Outraged, she thrust out her small, beautifully moulded chin. 'My name is Faith Charteris,' she said angrily. 'And I think we've already been introduced ... Remember, I was with your First Officer, Luke Webb.'

'Were you really!' There was something almost sinister about his lowered tone. A footstep in the passage outside made him open the door and shout authoritatively, 'You there, tell the First Mate I want him here at once!'

Aware of the Captain's harsh eyes upon her still, Faith merely shrugged her shoulders. She would not, could not appear to be afraid. In a short time she heard Luke's sharp, quick steps on the alley outside and she drew back, holding her breath in suspense.

'Come and look in here, Mr Mate,' the Captain called to him. 'I think you'll be interested.'

Puzzled, Luke peered into the cabin, then he started back in astonishment. 'Faith!' he choked. 'What the devil are you doing here?'

'That's what I want to know, Mr Mate. I've asked her, but the girl seems to have lost her tongue.'

'Luke!' Faith whispered. 'I'm sorry. I didn't want you to be involved ... I couldn't tell you ...'

'Tell me what?' Luke asked, staring hard at Faith and then back at the Captain in a puzzled, helpless way. 'I don't understand.'

'You seem to understand little, Mr Mate,' the Captain went on in an impatient tone. 'But then I've been at sea a long time. I know the waterfronts.'

'Sir——' Luke choked with embarrassment. 'Sir, it's not like that at all. I thought Faith had gone back with the launch.' He moistened his lips and turned troubled eyes to her. 'What made you do this?' he asked in a shattered tone. 'What happened?'

The Captain flicked his dark eyes in her direction and just for a moment Faith thought he was going to strike her. She stared back at him as defiantly as she could. 'Luke happens to be telling the truth. He knew nothing about this. I didn't tell him.'

'Then you're with Tan Chow?'

'No!' Faith turned sharply away from him.

'Sir! If I could speak to you alone.' Luke sounded desperate.

The Captain ignored him and remained standing just inside the cabin door, his gaze still upon Faith. He expected to be answered. She thought of Jeremy and her firmly moulded chin rose again. Her grey-blue eyes met the Captain's as she told him, 'I stowed away on your ship because I must get to Bali.' She thought quickly, realising that she must not implicate Tan Chow. 'Your First Mate knew nothing of my scheme, and Tan Chow was telling the truth too. I did give him a shock.'

An uneasy silence filled the cabin for a few moments. Then the Captain laughed shortly. 'So you're all on your own and on your way to Bali?'

Faith nodded, but she was shivering again. She did not like the way Captain Hilliard was smiling. She closed her eyes and swayed a little. Luke's protest was like a mumble from a mile away. As darkness closed upon her she heard the Captain's voice commanding, 'Don't faint here. There'll be no one to look after you on the *English Rose*. And I'm afraid you have a long voyage ahead. We're certainly not going to Bali!'

CHAPTER TWO

Not going to Bali! The news had torn Faith apart and for a long time, in the semi-darkness of the cabin, she sat hunched up on the hard floorboards, a sorry, bedraggled figure, her head lowered in desolation.

Where were they going? Tan Chow had said Bali and so had Luke. With a gnawing sense of fear in her stomach, Faith stretched out her cramped legs. The Captain had made it plain that he had no interest, no sympathy whatever, in her as a woman. He had been both insulting and sarcastic. She supposed that she was an embarrassment to him. But she was doing no real harm. She was by no means the kind of girl *he* had imagined her to be.

She grew hot with indignation as she struggled to her feet and glanced fearfully at the ceiling. With narrowed eyes she tried to pierce the grey light. She crossed unsteadily to the porthole and raising herself on tiptoe stared out into what looked like another vast and even more frightening world. Her eyes grew limpid with wonder. One day at sea had left the south-west monsoon far behind and now it was night and in the soft darkness the sea was eerily silent and studded with a myriad bright reflected stars. So many stars! There was nothing else; no

horizon, no white curling waves, only a vast empti-
ness and the sparkling communication from millions
of other similar lonesome planets.

Overwhelmed, locked in loneliness, Faith turned
back into her small cell and bravely fought back her
tears. Never had she known such isolation. It was
like awakening in space—a space that stretched to
eternity and held no other soul in it.

She jerked to attention again, listened. Music!
Her heart began to beat fast again. It was Indian
music and it drifted through the porthole. So often
on the Singapore quay she had paused to listen to
the insistent, rhythmic sound of sitar and drum coming over the water from the deep sea vessels. So there
were Indians on board. The crew was not entirely
made up of Chinese and Malays. Only a Hindu
could evoke such longing. She closed her eyes again,
and listening, sighed deeply into the abyss of nos-
talgia.

Her slim body grew taut as a new fear leapt into
her grey eyes. Surely the *English Rose* was not on
her way to Rangoon or Calcutta? Could it be that
she was sailing further and further away from
Jeremy?

The sound of music was abruptly cut out by a
sudden outburst of voices and then, curiously, all
was silent again. With strained ears, Faith listened
intently. 'Batten all ports!' she heard someone yell,
and that was all. The silence returned and with it
an uncanny hush. She closed her eyes and leant back
against the cabin door. A numb fatalism seemed to

be creeping over her. Something was wrong, she could feel it in her bones, but she did not care. A squall and a stiff breeze that whisked up the sea had not worried her, but this silky silence was different. She straightened up and listened again. It *was* unnerving. She suddenly wanted to scream out, do anything to break the silence. 'Luke!' she called in a quavering voice. 'Luke!' she faltered again through trembling lips ... But she knew very well that Luke would not hear her.

There was nothing she could do. She could shout and shout and no one would come—the dark Captain would see to that. She climbed up on to the rubber-lined bunk and tried to calm herself by thinking of Jeremy. With glistening eyes she remembered his last words. 'Darling,' he had promised, 'we're going to England. We're going to live in an English village. We're not going to dream of a white Christmas, Faith—we're going to have one. I don't intend to stay at sea. I'm going to stay with you, my darling.'

She covered her face with her hands and thought of Jeremy again. 'Oh, where are you?' she whispered brokenly into the darkness. 'Oh, Jeremy, where have you gone?'

Then her expression changed to one of bitter contempt as she thought of Luke Webb. What was he doing? Surely he was not afraid of the Captain? Even though he was dwarfed by his Captain, he could surely stand up to him on her behalf? *She* was not afraid of Captain Hilliard; she just hated him. She had never ever met such an ill-mannered and brutal man, she decided. There was something terrifying about his behaviour and his appearance. Was Luke really going to allow him to keep her locked up? Surely it was against the law for someone to keep her imprisoned against her will?

Exhaustion and outrage finally drove her into a troubled sleep. She dreamt that a black rat was chasing her and that she was cornered. Shuddering violently, she awoke and, remembering the ghastly details of her dream, did her best to calm herself with the knowledge that a Hindu dream man had once told her that dreams always meant the reverse. She would escape, she thought determinedly. She would not be trapped for long. She would get to Bali somehow; she would find Jeremy. Surely that was what her dream had meant?

With a fresh spurt of confidence, she climbed down from her bunk bed and crossed lightly to the porthole. It was almost light and she noticed the parcel of food which Tan Chow had brought her lying in the wash-basin. No, she decided, drawing her gaze forcibly from it, she was not that hungry yet. She peered out of the porthole. It was barely dawn; the great golden sun was still heaving itself out of the vast deep. But there was nothing odd about that. It was the fact that the whole crew seemed to be on deck and alerted that made Faith catch her breath in alarm. She recalled the earlier cry of 'Batten all ports!' and now a new and more ghastly apprehension filled her. She stared out again. The sea was as flat as mercury, there was not a breath of wind. The men were very busy lashing everything down. And in a flash, Faith knew. A typhoon was coming!

And in the emergency she had been forgotten.

Within half an hour Faith knew that her assumption had been correct. It was morning, but the sun had been swallowed at birth by the brooding dark clouds. The last breath of air seemed to have been squeezed from the cabin. Yet somewhere she knew that a mighty wind was getting up; she could hear it proclaiming its coming above the shouting and hammering on deck. The men were excited, agitated. It could mean disaster; caught in the eye of a typhoon, even a well-found ship had no chance of escape.

Surely they did not mean to leave her locked up here by herself? They could not be so cruel, so insensitive. But no one came to her aid and ten minutes later the ship began to rise and fall and she knew that the glass-like surface of the sea was breaking up. The moaning wind seemed to suddenly reach gale force and scream like a thousand demons. Faith's blood ran cold at the sound of it and with clenched teeth she hung on to the wash-basin as the ship began to pitch and toss.

She was really scared and trembling. In a sudden fit of panic she shouted as hard as she could, 'Luke! Luke!' She braced her legs stiffly as she fought to keep her balance and shouted again, desperately, 'Luke! Luke!'

But Luke did not come and the *English Rose* began to rear crazily. Faith found herself screaming, 'Captain Hilliard! Captain Hilliard!'

The Captain did not come to her aid either and, managing to grab the porthole handle, she raised herself up so that she could peer out. This time she fell back, shocked, grey. The waves were black, curling and dangerous. She tried to batten the porthole, but she was not strong enough. Even as she tried a deluge of spray caught her and hurled her to the floor.

'Luke! Luke!' She sobbed the name and then lay silent in the salt water, soaked to the skin, beaten.

One deluge followed another and Faith knew that it was useless to shout. With a tremendous effort of will she fought against the lashing spray and after hauling herself up with the aid of the basin, she struggled across to the bunk. She was terrified, but she managed to clamber up and topple over on to the hard bunk bed. It's like a coffin, she thought with a fresh rush of fright. It may well be my coffin. Then the *English Rose* was caught broadside on and she heard only the crack of her head as she was hurled over and crashed against the cabin wall.

Later, when the frenzied waters were at peace and the demons exorcised, she opened her eyes. One side of her face was terribly painful and she found it difficult to open her right eye. She moved a little and, catching her breath with pain, thought her ribs were broken, but she was too exhausted to care. She lay with her eyes closed and even when the cabin door opened and she heard voices, she kept perfectly still. Mentally and physically she was beaten.

She recognised Luke's voice. He sounded shocked as he spoke to the person with him.

'God! Are we really responsible for this?'

Yes, you are, Faith thought, but she had not the energy to speak and remained still and silent.

Then she heard the Captain's harsh voice. 'You'd better tidy her up, Mr Mate. And the cabin.'

Faith felt herself losing consciousness, but something in the Captain's hard cruel tone made her fight to retain her senses. Her cold lips stirred for the first time ... with unmitigated scorn and disdain.

The Captain's voice came again, no less harshly this time. 'Pull yourself together, Mr Mate. A few bruises won't kill a girl like that. In fact a shake-up might well put some sense into her foolish head. She'll not try for a cheap trip again.' And after a pause, 'She hadn't even the sense to batten the port-hole. There'll be some baling out to do in here.'

'She looks very ill, sir.' Luke's voice shook.

'Did you expect her to look as though she'd been on holiday?'

'I think she's injured, sir ...'

Hearing the rustle of oilskins and the swish of water, Faith quickly turned her head to the wall, wincing in pain as she did so. She kept her eyes tightly shut.

'It's no use turning away, Miss ... whatever your name may be, I've forgotten. You couldn't get away from us now however hard you tried.'

'Go away,' Faith whispered. 'Go away. I don't want to look at you.' She knew she sounded pathetic, but she could not stop her words.

'You're not exactly a pretty sight yourself, Miss Charteris.' He remembered her name this time. 'You look as if someone's beaten you up.'

The Captain's tone was coldly mocking and Faith turned slowly to focus her one open eye hard upon him. Her lips were tightly compressed. Something cool was pressed to her lips and in a deep, authoritative tone the Captain was ordering, 'Drink it. I promise it won't poison you.' And then, in a gentler voice, 'I'm not quite the demon I look, you know.'

Painfully, choking a little, Faith managed to swallow a little liquid from the flask. After a few sips she began to feel a little better. She tried to open her swollen eye and found that she could not; the pain was too great. Again she fell back. 'Go away,' she whispered, feeling sorry for herself again. 'Just leave me alone.'

'Give her the rest, Mr Mate.'

Faith heard the Captain's voice fading out and then Luke's coming in with, 'Sir, I couldn't touch her.' And with rising alarm, 'I daren't.'

'Is she so fragile?' There was faint amusement in the Captain's words. 'Very well then,' he said, 'leave her to me.'

Faith felt the flask being pressed more firmly to her lips this time. A large, hard hand raised her head a little.

'Accept it as a tribute to your courage, Miss Charteris,' he said sarcastically. 'A black eye never killed anyone,' he went on sharply. 'You're not going to die, you know.'

In a frenzy of fury, Faith raised her hand and knocked the flask out of the Captain's hand. She raised herself up and called wretchedly to Luke.

Beside himself with relief at the return of Faith's strength, Luke moved clumsily forward and seized her hand, and she exclaimed in pain.

Captain Hilliard moved Luke forcibly to one side. 'stand back. Do you want to kill the girl?' He gave Luke another savage glance. 'Let this be a lesson to you, Mr Mate,' he continued. 'If you don't know how to look after a woman, keep away from them—or at least confine your amorous activities ashore. I haven't time for this sort of nonsense ... nor the inclination.'

Through a haze of nausea, Faith was aware that strong arms were easing her up and she realised that she was being carried, and with the utmost care, out of the cabin. Somewhere in the background Luke was calling in a distressed voice, 'Take her to my cabin, sir!'

'Not a chance!' The Captain's voice was like an icy blast across Faith's still face. 'We're only three days from Labuan and I intend to have this young woman fit enough to leave my ship by that time.'

Opening her one good eye a little, Faith winced again at the pain, and then again, but this time at the threat of invincible power she saw in the dark, burning eyes above her. She saw too how his full, well-formed mouth dragged down at the corners, hard and unyielding.

Luke was calling again, 'She's weak, sir. She looks

dreadful. Her bones must be bruised.'

'Either that or broken,' the Captain agreed. 'Don't stand there like an idiot, Mr Mate. Open the door. There's no need to look so desperate. I may not be the sensitive type, but I can treat a black eye and a few bruises. And remember, Mr Mate, that if I hadn't had the foresight to lock this woman in the cabin, she might well have been struggling in the sea ... instead of in my arms.'

Faith lay limp again, helpless. So that was why she had been locked in the cabin! Involuntarily she turned her face to the Captain's dark jacket and for a moment she listened to the heavy, powerful thud of his heart. Then she felt herself being put down gently upon a cool, soft bed. She looked up and saw his dark eyes close to her own, then the pain came back and she knew no more.

When she opened her eyes again she felt the Captain's arm supporting her. 'I think I'm going to die,' she whispered. 'I feel dreadful.'

'No one is going to die on my ship,' the Captain told her brusquely. 'No, you're not going to die, Miss Charteris. I have a feeling that you're going to live and cause me quite a bit of trouble.'

Faith closed her eyes again. Luke returned and, as she felt the flask being held to her lips again, she spluttered and gasped pathetically.

'Faith,' Luke began desperately, 'you're going to be all right. You've just been shaken up ...'

His voice faded out and the Captain spoke again. 'You've had quite a battering and you don't look your best, Miss Charteris. But if Mr Mate will kindly fetch me some water and a face cloth and towel, I may well be able to tidy you up.'

'I'll do that, sir. I'll bathe her face.'

'Since when have you been giving orders on this ship, Mr Mate?' The Captain's voice rose authoritatively. 'Will you please get that bowl of water. I haven't all day, damn you!'

For the first time Luke held his ground. 'You don't understand, sir. Faith's a decent type of girl. I've known her for some time. I don't want you to embarrass her.'

'Hasn't she embarrassed me?' The Captain sounded contemptuous. 'Get yourself a drink, Mr Mate,' he ordered Luke. 'You look as though you need one. Leave this to me.'

'I'll get the water ...' Luke staggered away almost drunkenly to the adjoining room, but before he could reach it, Faith had struggled up and called, 'Luke!'

'Go on!' The Captain waved him on with an authoritative gesture of his hand. 'We're waiting.'

A few minutes later Luke returned with the necessary requisites and with shaking hands set them down on the small bedside table.

The Captain did not bother to look up. He was studying the girl in his bed more intently. 'She's not very old,' he remarked grimly as his dark eyes ran assessingly over Faith. 'No more than twenty, I would say. Do you know much about her, Mr Mate? Other than that she has the usual feminine attributes?'

'Sir, I assure you ...'

The Captain's low laugh cut mockingly across Luke's adamant words. 'The same old hard luck story.' He laughed out again, adding coldly, 'I don't believe it.'

'Faith has a respectable job in a shipping office, sir. She shares a bungalow with another girl.'

'You'd better get to the bridge, Mr Mate,' the Captain ordered with a sudden impatience. Then he stood up and threw off his oilskin jacket and glanced significantly at the door. 'This won't take long,' he said, and frowned back at Luke. 'Don't worry,' he laughed again, 'I'm old enough to be the girl's father, Mr Mate—or at least I feel like it. I could quite easily give her a sound thrashing ... which she certainly deserves.'

'Sir ...' Luke's face had turned white with alarm. 'Sir ...'

With a flick of his strong brown hand the Captain dismissed him.

The first thing Faith saw when she awoke in the middle of the night was the glittering electric light bulb, and then she remembered that she was no longer a prisoner in the empty cabin. She still ached in every limb, but her mind was clearing. She felt cool, almost calm. Opening one good eye and half of the other, she saw that she was lying in a bed and that she was wearing a very fine silk pyjama jacket —an enormous jacket.

Where was her dress? She moved a little and whimpered faintly. Almost immediately she heard the scrape of a chair across the floor and the sound of a door opening. When she looked up again, she saw the huge shape of the Captain looming over her, and she drew a sharp breath. He was wearing a midnight blue silk kimono now and there was a trace of glistening perspiration above his upper lip. His face was still fierce, but there was an intensity of expression in his coffee-brown eyes that made Faith's heart instantly beat fast. He was concerned for her! The very idea made her feel strange.

'Do you usually batter your stowaways almost to death?' she asked with an effort.

Ignoring her words, he asked flatly, 'Would you like a cigarette? Or a drink?'

She shook her head. 'I don't smoke,' she whispered, feeling her helplessness again.

'Good! I wouldn't really care to risk having my ship set on fire.'

Staring at the long sleeves of her jacket, Faith fought back with, 'You could always lock me up again ...'

'And roast you?' The Captain's face grew dark, his eyes glinted. 'Not likely, Miss Charteris.'

Weakly she glared back at him.

'That cabin was the safest place on the ship for you during the typhoon,' he told her as he loomed over her again. 'Just be thankful that you weren't washed overboard. You weren't invited to make this trip, Miss Charteris.' As he spoke the Captain's eyes glinted angrily and he reached for one of his own cigars and lit it. 'Would you,' he asked, staring down at her again, 'like to have been torn to pieces by the sharks?'

'You sounded as though you yourself would like to tear me to pieces.' Faith's voice was full of self-pity again.

'Don't be childish.' For a few moments he paced the floor, then he flung disdainfully, 'Although I hardly expect you to be anything else. Intelligent women do not stow away on ships.'

Faith felt a wave of weakness engulf her again. 'I'm sorry,' she whispered, and turned her cheek on to the cool pillow. 'I didn't expect to cause all this trouble. I thought it was just a case of slipping on and slipping off . . .'

'Just like the knitting you should have stuck to, Miss Charteris. As simple as that, I see.' His lips curled with scorn, but then he frowned at the small figure in the large bed again.

Then she faltered, 'I would like a cup of tea. I'd be grateful.' Her eyes grew soft with entreaty.

'I'll get some for you. Then you can tell me what made you so sure we were going to Bali.'

Faith managed to focus him clearly with her good eye. 'Is this your bedroom?' she asked in a small voice. 'Am I in your bed?'

'Of course it's my bed,' he told her. 'And I'll be damned glad when you can get out of it.'

'Thank you.'

Something in her tone made the Captain turn back to scrutinise her frowningly, then with an angry, impatient noise he strode quickly from the bedroom.

He returned very soon with a tray and a pot of tea and set it down on the built-in locker at the side of the bed. Faith took a beaker from him without a word, but after a few heartening sips she smiled up at him and asked in a stiff little voice, 'Were you speaking the truth when you said you weren't sailing to Bali?'

Standing back on his heels for a moment, Captain Hilliard scowled and tightened the belt of his silk kimono. 'I have my orders, Miss Charteris,' he told her coldly. 'I'm not usually asked to disclose them.'

She nodded meekly. She did not want to antagonise him again so soon. She had to think of Jeremy—and Tan Chow. She would not involve the Chinese; he had at least given her a lead. Somehow she had to find out just where they were going, but she would keep her thoughts to herself for the time being.

'Why are you so desperate to get to Bali?' the Captain enquired, studying her with narrowed eyes as though he could read what was going on in her mind. 'Are you running away from someone? The police, perhaps?' He raised one thick, bushy eyebrow. 'Are you in trouble, Miss Charteris?'

Faith's heart leapt. She was not in trouble; but Jeremy was, and for his sake she had to be careful. 'What kind of trouble?' she asked hesitantly.

'The kind of trouble girls are idiotic enough to get themselves into. You'll not be the first one, Miss Charteris.'

'I am certainly not in that kind of trouble,' she told him with a rush of annoyance, and she stared hard at the beaker which shook in her trembling hands. 'I acted on an impulse,' she told him, acting on one again. 'I wanted a change, and I'd had Denpasar in mind for some time. The place is whirling with tourists and I thought I might easily get a job there. I'm sick of the shipping office, sick of typing and fed up with Singapore. It's as simple as that.'

'I see. And you had no money at all?'

'I'm tired,' she whispered, evading the question. 'I want to sleep—my head is aching. I'm just sorry I'm in your bed.'

'I'm sorry too.' Something in his mocking tone made Faith sink back on to her pillow. 'We're due at the island of Labuan in three days and I intend to land you there, Miss Charteris. A schooner will take you back to Singapore. They hug the coast and take some time, but that doesn't concern me. You won't run the danger of meeting another typhoon.'

Or another cold-blooded, inhuman Captain, Faith thought as she lay very still. She made no comment and eventually she heard Captain Hilliard's feet moving over the floor and the door shut. Then tears welled into her eyes and poured down on to her pillow. Labuan! She had heard of the place; it was a small native community; there were only a few whites. It was a copra island just off the mainland of Borneo and the last place she wanted to see. Some of the ships back in the port of Singapore were loaded with copra from Labuan.

So she was to be landed on the small island and left there to wait for a schooner. The idea made her sit up with alarm. She refused to be pushed off at any old place, she absolutely refused. Wincing, she pushed back her sheets and eased herself on to the side of the bed. There was no time to lose. She had to get some strength. And she had to get to the bathroom!

Dizzily, she stepped out, alarmingly aware of her lack of trousers, but thankful for the length of the Captain's blue silk jacket. She felt weak but determined, and she kept her good eye on the door opposite. With her chin up she felt as though she was wading through water. She managed well until she reached the middle of the room, then she felt the floor move beneath her and she began to sway dangerously. Fighting for control, she glanced down and saw for the first time the severe bruising on her slim legs. The deep purple patches made her feel sick. Looking up again, she caught sight of her distorted face in a wall mirror, and gave a cry of horror and dismay and her knees suddenly gave way. Frantically she searched for something to grip, but there was nothing ...

Captain Hilliard heard the dull thud and he was there in a few moments. He frowned heavily at the small crumpled heap on the floor, at the swirling mass of tawny hair, the white face and bruised carnation lips. With an involuntary action he stooped down and with a hand that was infinitely gentle he brushed a curtain of hair back from Faith's swollen brow.

Faith stirred, remembered the hideously swollen

face she had seen reflected in the mirror and covered her face with her hands. 'Thank you,' she sobbed almost hysterically.

'I thought you'd fainted.' His voice was crushing again.

'I lost my balance, that's all.'

'Then we'll see that you don't this time,' he said as he swept her up into his arms and carried her across the room. 'I take it you were on your way to the bathroom.'

Faith wanted to say something, but her lips merely quivered as though they had offered some quick prayer. She felt the comforting strength of his arm beneath her shoulder blades, the silk beneath her own satin-smooth calves. Again she turned her face to him. His kimono had a faintly spicy smell and she moved her cheek across it.

It was this gesture that Captain Hilliard caught reflected in the wall mirror and for a moment his breath was held in his throat. He glared into the mirror ... the hostile glare of a man suddenly invaded by an army of unexpected and unwanted ideas.

Faith felt the surge of his great chest and one of her arms rose to curl about his neck. Then he was saying shortly, 'I'll put you down here. There's a chair—you'll be able to manage.' And closing the bathroom door after him he called, 'If you want anything, shout. I'll be right outside.'

Inside the small room Faith shivered and glanced at the door again. Then, confidently, she took a step towards the wash-basin. The cool water made her feel better. And, strangely enough, so did the Captain's obvious, if reluctant, concern. For a moment an odd little smile played about her mouth. She tried to stand up straight, and got yet another shock as she came face to face with her reflection in the mirror above the basin. She gave a little gasp of horror; she could hardly recognise herself. One side of her face was badly swollen and cruelly distorted. Her brow was bruised and she had a black eye—and as for her hair, it was like a golden brown, tattered shawl about her shoulders. She stared at herself again and then covered her face with her hands. It would never be the same again, she thought, and she began to sob a little. If she did find Jeremy, he would not recognise her.

She did not hear the door open, but she did feel the Captain's hand as he reached out to grip her arm. She turned to him, dismay in her eyes.

'Now don't start worrying about your face,' the Captain told her with rough sympathy. He added with a short laugh, 'You won't have much competition on Labuan. The island is slowly being depopulated.'

'I'll go back to bed,' Faith whispered, not caring how cruel he was now. 'I'm beginning to float again. And believe me, Captain, I don't want either your sarcasm or pity. I'd just like you to help me back to bed.'

'My bed!'

'Any bed,' Faith whispered, as he gathered her up

into his arms and carried her back to the bedroom.

'Mr Mate is waiting to see you,' he told her. 'That should cheer you.' He peered down at her white face for a moment and frowned into the pained eyes, then he laughed. 'There's no reason why you should like me, Miss Charteris,' he said with a new quiet certainty. 'But try not to look quite so contemptuous. I am trying to help you, you know.'

Faith drew down her swollen eyelids and tried hard to think of Jeremy. She was doing all this for him, she told herself. She was suffering for him both pain and humiliation. But even as these thoughts moved unsteadily through her brain she was much more conscious of the Captain's strong physical presence. His words were harsh, but he had given her his bed ... even his silk pyjamas. He sounded cruel, but he had also been kind. What was more alarming was the fact that it seemed so nice, so completely natural to be in his arms. She raised her head a little and gave him a funny little distorted smile. For the moment she was content to let him take charge of her.

CHAPTER THREE

FIVE minutes after Captain Hilliard had gone back to the bridge there was a tap on the cabin door.

'Come in,' Faith called in a small voice. She knew it would be Luke and she was anxious to see him. She smiled when she saw him coming in with a sheepish look on his lean face. He wore white drill trousers and an open-necked white shirt. His cap was stuck back on his head at a jaunty angle. She thought he looked a little flushed, as though he had just lost his temper with someone, but he grinned as usual and teased, 'Well, now, this must be a turn-up for the old man's log. July the fifth ... rare bird in bunk.' His dark eyes flicked over Faith as she sat propped up against her pillows. 'And what are a few bruises, anyhow!'

'I don't think I like that,' she said, staring hard at him and remembering how squeamish he actually was.

Luke sat on the foot of the bed twirling his cap in his hands. 'No offence,' he said with a grin. 'It's just strange to see a girl in the Captain's suite. He's a loner, you know—oh, he likes women in their proper place, but that's not on his ship.' Luke stopped playing with his cap and his eyes grew a little more sober. 'You look very much better this morning,' he said thoughtfully. 'I can see that the old man has been looking after you.'

'Must you call him an old man?' Faith swallowed hard, wondering why she felt so put out. Then she laughed a little and said, 'Captain Hilliard's an odd man, but not an old one.'

'It's just a term, darling.' Luke's face broke into a grin again. 'Still, it must be a new experience for him. You never know, Faith, you might rouse that protective instinct yet.'

'You do talk rubbish, Luke.' Faith looked away and then back again at him, saying, 'And I don't happen to be what you would call an experience. I'm a nuisance to the man, that's all. And he doesn't mind telling me so, either.'

'You're a bit of a novelty, then ...'

'Oh, for goodness' sake, Luke! You're making me tired. Must you go on about the man?'

'Perhaps I'm jealous?' Playfully he threw his cap into the air and caught it again. 'I could be.' He threw it again. 'I should be.' His dark eyes glinted.

'Don't be ridiculous. You know you're not.'

The cap was still in Luke's hands now. 'Tell me,' he said, and he searched Faith's face now, 'why did you do it? You made quite a fool of me, you know.'

'Perhaps I couldn't bear to be parted from you, Luke.'

'Now who's being ridiculous?'

She sighed and then told him more seriously, 'I'm going to Bali, Luke. The Captain is going to put me off at Labuan, so I'll have to wait until I can get a ship from there. But I must get there. I must get to Bali. I'm not going back to Singapore.'

Luke stood up. 'To hell with Bali,' he burst out suddenly. 'It's all right if you're a tourist, Faith, but you don't want to work there, surely? You're much better off in Singapore.'

'You told me that the *English Rose* was sailing to Bali. That's why I stayed on the ship, Luke. I'm determined to get there.'

Luke stroked the back of his brown neck and made no comment. Then his eye fell upon the compress lying on the bed. 'Is that supposed to be on your eye?' he asked her.

'Yes,' Faith answered him in a clipped voice. 'Captain Hilliard is coming back to change it. He may be an old man, but he at least knows how to deal with a black eye.'

'And a young girl, so it seems. I must say I'm amazed. Although it could be his paternal instinct. Would you say he was a father figure, Faith?'

Faith bowed her head. 'I wish you would go,' she said in a tired voice. 'I'm in no mood for jokes, Luke. But don't worry about me, I'm all right.'

'Perhaps I should worry about the old man, then. He doesn't look as though he's had much sleep.' Luke stuck his peaked cap on his head again.

'How old are you?' Faith asked, her heart beating fast again for no apparent reason.

'I'm twenty-four,' Luke tossed back. 'The Captain's thirty at least. So you see, we're both getting on a bit.'

For no reason again there was a smile on Faith's lips, but she said nothing.

'Yes, he's a strange chap,' Luke said, thinking the smile was for him. 'And he's clever.' His gaze travelled to the wall stacked with books. 'I've never really understood him, though.'

Faith watched him return to the door where the sunlight caught him. He blazed in light and, staring at him, she thought how lithe and dark and handsome he was. But his features were just a little finely drawn. Considering him, she noted the weakness in his face. He had merry, kindly eyes, and she liked him. But not enough to confide in him, she decided quickly. Luke had not a strong character, just a nice one.

Then to Faith's surprise Tan Chow appeared soundlessly with a tray in his hands. He approached her, his parchment face breaking into what was meant to be an encouraging smile. 'Missy take breakfast?' he asked in his strange broken English. 'Coffee and rolls. Egg light boil?'

She nodded stiffly and her gaze stretched out to Luke.

He came back and said abruptly, 'All right, Tan Chow, I'll take that. You can go.'

Faith's eyes stayed on the tray until the Chinese had gone like a shadow, then she glanced up at Luke. 'He scared me before,' she said through trembling lips. 'I don't know why ...'

'I don't know why either. The old devil seems to like you, Faith.' He forced a laugh this time. 'But who wouldn't?' he teased again. 'Even bruised.'

'I'll be all right now. And I expect I'll soon be turfed out into that empty cabin again, Luke. Come and see me then. Fortunately it's only three days to Labuan.'

'Why did you do it?' Luke asked again, and looking up, Faith saw that his merry eyes had lost their brightness. 'You seemed to like your job in Singapore. You liked the bungalow, and Monique. I think there's something you haven't told me, Faith.'

'Of course there is,' she fought back impatiently. 'And I don't intend to. This venture of mine has absolutely nothing to do with you, Luke. You don't need to worry.'

'But I am worried.'

'Are you?' She reached out with an impulsive warmth to touch Luke's hand. 'We've always been good friends,' she told him, then she gave his hand a playful tug. 'You know very well, Luke, that you never take a girl seriously.'

Luke shuffled with embarrassment. 'Maybe,' he said, but there was a curious glint in his eyes as he studied her for a few moments. 'Maybe not,' he added in a more reflective tone.

Faith was glad to see the door open and Tan Chow come in again. She stared at him in surprise. 'Good heavens!' she said. 'I haven't started,' and glancing at Luke, 'I'll see you later, Luke. I really must eat something.'

Luke took his cue and strode to the door, but not before he had exerted his authority with, 'Mind you look after the young lady, Tan Chow.'

'Tan Chow do that.' The Chinese glanced furtively back at Luke and then he was smiling again
at Faith. 'Egg good, missy? Tan Chow pour coffee?
Yes?'

'I can manage, thank you, Tan Chow. Come back
later. I can't rush.'

'Velly well, missy. Missy much better?'

'Very much better, thank you,' Faith returned in
a staccato voice. 'And you can go now, Tan Chow.'

He would not go, and Faith eyed him warily; a
hundred accusations thundering in her brain. 'You
told me that the *English Rose* was going to Bali,' she
said in an undertone. 'Why did you deceive me, Tan
Chow? You won't get away with it, you know. I'll
just have to inform the Captain.'

'Missy, missy!' Tan Chow gestured wildly with
his square yellow hand. 'Do not say such things. We
go to Bali. Tan Chow not lie—you see.'

'We happen to be going to Labuan, which is off
Borneo, Tan Chow. The Captain told me so.'

Tan Chow was not perturbed. 'Yes, yes,' he agreed
hastily. 'We go to Labuan, then we go to Bali.
Always the same trip, missy. You see Labuan, then
you see Bali. Tan Chow speak truth.'

Faith swallowed hard as she stared at him. Could
he be speaking the truth? Could she believe him?
With all her heart she wanted to. 'You're sure?' she
whispered, leaning forward over the tray a little.
'You're absolutely sure, Tan Chow?'

Tan Chow shrugged his slight shoulders. 'Always
the same, missy—you see.'

Alone again, Faith felt her heart rise and sink like an anchor again. Was Captain Hilliard being sadistically perverse? Was he taking some delight in watching her squirm? He knew that she was desperate to get to Bali. And if his ship was going there why had he decided to put her off at the island of Labuan? She thought of Jeremy again, of his suffering, the torture of mind that she knew he must be enduring, and in a moment she knew that she must get down on her knees and beg the Captain to allow her to stay on the *English Rose*. She would offer to work her passage. She could cook; she would do anything. If he still tried to force her ashore, she would kick and scream. She had to get to Jeremy. She would suffer any humiliation to do so.

Jeremy! With a great surge of emotion, Faith dropped back against her pillows. She wondered if he was thinking of her just as she was thinking of him. Her throat filled up and tears oozed stingingly into her bruised face. She patted them away with the back of her hand and then closed her eyes. Soon snow was falling, falling softly and silently and like wood ash, just as Jeremy had said it would. They were together in England ... together, happy ...

She slept for three hours and awoke with a rush of anxiety. Struggling up, she reached out nervously for the compress and got it back into position just before the Captain strode into the room. He stood at the foot of the bed, unsmiling, his dark eyes upon her. 'You can take that compress off,' he said in a harsh voice. 'I'll fix another. The swelling has gone down.'

'Thank you.' The knowledge that she must go down on her knees to the man once again made her uneasy. 'I'm feeling much better. I could go back to my ... the other cabin now.'

'You'll be back there tonight,' he said sharply, turning away from her still, earnest face. 'They're fixing it up now.'

Faith caught her breath. In horror she stared back at him. She had said she could go back, not that she wanted to. The very idea filled her with horror. 'Must I?' she whispered, and moistened her lips in a gesture of desperation. 'I didn't like it.'

He clasped his brown hands together and rubbed them as though he was cold. 'I prefer this one myself,' he said, unsmiling. 'But then I do happen to be Captain of this ship.'

The compress dropped from Faith's eye once again and she picked it up and threw it down the bed. 'Please,' she entreated him, 'please let me stay here.'

Captain Hilliard took a few slow steps towards her. 'I didn't think you were the nervous type,' he said. 'It takes guts to stow away on a ship. Either that or you're an idiot.'

'I'm an idiot,' she returned swiftly, thinking of the dark cabin again.

'Are you nervous of me, Miss Charteris?'

She stared up at him, then she turned her head away from him as she said, 'Sometimes I am. But you have been kind. I'm grateful ... especially for the compress.'

'Nonsense, Miss Charteris. Don't run away with
the idea that I'm kind. I'm a hard man, but a practical one. I'm making sure that you'll be fit enough
to leave my ship at Labuan, that's all. Try to rest
now,' he said, and strode away to the door.

Faith turned her face into the pillow, then she
stirred again. The Captain was calling to her again
from somewhere beyond the door. 'It's all right,
Miss Charteris, you can stay where you are until we
reach the island. I'll sleep in the other cabin.'

'Thank you ... thank you.'

The room darkened a little and she saw that the
Captain was filling the doorway again. She sat up
just a little because she thought he was going to
smile. She was sure he was going to smile. But he
did not; he just kept standing there, staring at her,
until she said in desperation, 'Could I have my dress
and sandals, please? I'm going to try to get up.'

'Certainly.' He turned to go. 'I'll ask Tan Chow
to get them.'

'Captain Hilliard!'

He turned back again, frowning.

Faith stared back at him and suddenly her heart
was hammering again. His eyes were too deep, too
steady, the line of his jaw too powerful. She managed to smile a little, but that was all; her parted
lips pressed together again and she lowered her eyelids. Whatever she had been going to ask, she had
forgotten.

Tan Chow arrived ten minutes later with her
clothes. Her dress and tights had been washed and

she was genuinely pleased. Tan Chow had also brought her handbag. She took it from him and thanked him quickly. Tan Chow slipped away like a shadow again and two minutes later Faith was on her feet. This time she smiled; she felt quite steady.

By evening she felt that she was almost back to normal and she even hummed to herself as she stood eyeing herself in the wall mirror. Her face was still swollen badly on one side and one of her eyes was still half closed, but she did feel better. She had brushed her hair and brightened her lips, put on her dress and now she was struggling with her sandals. She found it impossible to get them on, for they had shrunk badly, so it was in her bare feet that she advanced slowly to the Captain's office. She tapped at the door, and leaning forward, peered into the room. It was almost like a sitting room, but there was a large desk and she saw that the Captain was sitting beside it. 'Captain Hilliard!' she called, peering a little further in this time and seeing him look up in surprise. 'I'm feeling much better. Could I walk out on the deck for a short time? It's so stiflingly hot.'

Captain Hilliard stood up. 'I'd prefer it if you did not,' he said decisively. 'You're not on a cruise, Miss Charteris. I'd advise you to stay in your cabin.'

'But why not?' Faith moved towards him. 'I'm not a prisoner. You're not taking me to Alcatraz.'

Ignoring her words, he glowered down at her feet. 'Where are your sandals?' he asked quite sharply. 'Did you intend to go on deck like that?' He went on frowning at her long slim bronzed legs.

'My sandals have shrunk,' she told him.

'I see.'

'I'd like to go up on to the deck. I can't breathe.'

'The men are quiet,' he said, giving her a direct look. 'I don't want them aroused.'

'Aroused?' Faith blinked back at him. Then she pulled a face and with a shrug told him, 'I don't think I'm the type to arouse men, Captain Hilliard, and well you know it.'

He smiled faintly, as though he did not intend to commit himself. Then he suggested, 'If you must have air, then I'd better escort you. I have ten minutes or so to spare.'

She gave him a glance which was just as non-committal as his own and then walked ahead. They reached the well deck and for a while they stood in silence against the ship's rails staring out across the sea.

Faith was the first one to speak and she said, 'It's beautiful, isn't it? And the air!' She raised her hand as though to touch it. 'You can almost pick it up.' Forgetting her problems for a moment, she even laughed and snatched at the air with both hands this time.

A muscle of the Captain's cheek worked as he watched her. His eyes narrowed as though to hide their fascination. 'It's a mercy we're moving,' he said abruptly. 'It's stiflingly hot at anchor. I'm always glad to get to sea again.'

'I didn't think anything on earth could affect you, Captain Hilliard.' Faith found herself smiling.

'Anyway,' she went on, 'you must admit that the sea is a wonderful colour. It's just like jade.'

A steadying hand gripped her arm and she turned to meet the Captain's eyes in surprise. 'Don't worry,' she told him with emphasis, 'I don't intend to fall overboard. I'm still hoping that you'll take pity on me and take me to Bali.'

'Then you're an optimist,' he said, and though for a moment his strong brown hand rested on hers, his voice was impatient again. 'Don't count on me for anything, Miss Charteris, not even the very air you breathe. Come along now, I think you've had enough. And I certainly have something better to do.'

'I could work my passage to Bali,' she said quickly, before he could move. With hope in her heart she watched him out of the corner of her good eye.

'Not on my ship, Miss Charteris. Don't get any ideas. You leave my ship at Labuan. I'm not taking any passengers to Bali.'

'Then you are going there?' Her heart leapt up joyously. Tan Chow had not deceived her.

This time the Captain did not answer her. Instead he turned around to give his full attention to something else. 'I don't like that damned thumping,' he said, and swore angrily. 'Good God, don't tell me the engineers are in trouble again!'

'Will you please listen to me!' Frantically now, desperation in her eyes, Faith suddenly reached out and clutched at his arm. 'Haven't you any kindly feelings at all?' she burst out. 'Can't you see that I'm desperate? I must get to Bali—and I need help.'

Her voice broke and faded away as she whispered. 'I have no one ... and I'm not the kind of girl you imagine me to be.'

'You may be right. And so it's time you were back in bed.' Ignoring her plea, the Captain took her arm and led her back to his suite. 'You should be all right tomorrow,' he told her as he watched her flop limply down into a chair. 'But don't overdo it. I've told you, Miss Charteris, the moment we reach Labuan you leave this ship.' He strode away to the door which led to his own office. 'I have some papers to make out,' he said, glancing back at her. 'There are one or two questions I have to ask you.' And frowning, he asked, 'Whoever thought of giving you that ridiculous name?'

'Faith?' She thought of her parents and for a moment closed her eyes. 'It was my mother's choice,' she told him in a small but deliberate voice. 'She wanted me to have it ... faith in people.'

'And you find yourself sadly disillusioned, eh?'

She glanced up because she had the distinct impression that he was going to laugh sarcastically at her. But he was not laughing and for a few moments they surveyed each other in silence. Then Faith said, 'I'm going to bed. Will you please close the door after you.'

Frowningly, Captain Hilliard went on watching her for a moment or two. Then he nodded and turned away.

The door closed quietly after him and now Faith's face twisted furiously. She covered her face with her hands, and winced with pain. There was nothing she could do. Obviously Captain Hilliard was not the kind of man to allow any feelings of sentiment to complicate his austere and disciplined life. She found his cool, steady way of observing her unnerving. It would do her no good to get down on her knees to him. Wearily she took off her dress, and after pausing to frown at the enormous pyjama jacket he had given her, she put it on and climbed back into bed. For some time she lay thinking of Jeremy and of how she could possibly get to Bali, her small battered face an image of desolation.

The next day was grillingly hot. Luke came to take Faith for a short walk on deck and for a while they watched some shearwaters skimming the shimmering water. The birds were remarkable and their flight sheer poetry, but even then they could not focus Faith's interest. She glanced at Luke, who also looked worried and ill at ease. 'What's wrong now, Luke?' she asked.

'Nothing really,' he answered her slowly. 'It's just that I've been thinking.'

'There is something wrong, then,' she teased, but her face remained still and grave.

'I'm serious,' he told her, and he turned now to stare at her as though he was seeing her for the first time. 'And I'm worried about you, Faith. You bother me. For the first time I'm more concerned about you than I am about myself. Faith . . .'

His lean hand closed over her hands and with an impatient gesture she drew her own away. 'Don't worry too much,' she said with a forced laugh. 'I'm going to Bali, Luke. And I'm like you in many ways. I don't want any ties. It's nice having you for a friend, you know. You're fun.'

'Is that all?'

'Of course!'

'I do feel responsible for you in a way, Faith,' he went on. 'I'm not just a playboy.'

'Don't worry about me,' Faith told him, and for a moment she raised grave eyes. 'I can look after myself, Luke. I'm not afraid of your Captain. And I will get to Bali.'

Luke grinned, himself again. 'You're looking better,' he said. 'Not so puffy.' Inclining his head and squinting at her, he teased, 'You know, I think that black eye of yours did something to the old man. He's almost as restless as I am myself. I knew you'd arouse his paternal instinct . . . if nothing else.'

Faith stared hard at him. 'You couldn't be serious for five minutes, could you?' she said stingingly, and then without another word she turned and made her way as smartly as she could back to her bedroom. For a while she tried to find something to read, but she found that most of the Captain's books were beyond her and in the end she just sat on the chair and closed her eyes until Tan Chow brought her tea. He seemed unusually pleased and grinned all the time. Watching him, Faith again felt herself seized by a feeling of revulsion and suspicion. Still, the Chinese had not lied to her. They were going to Bali . . . at

least the *English Rose* was going there, whether she
went or not.

'Soon reach island, missy,' Tan Chow was saying.
'Tonight, maybe.'

Faith just nodded and then dismissed him with a
shrug. She drank her tea very slowly. Labuan, she
thought bitterly, that was where she was going. She
had wasted her time, and everyone else's. And she
was no closer to Jeremy. She was sailing further away
from him all the time; she felt the chill truth in her
bones.

At dusk the *English Rose* anchored off Labuan,
and unable to wait to see the island, Faith crept out
of her room in her bare feet and made her way up
on to the well deck again. She could see that they
had moored just off a coral cove and that the island
was ahead. As she stood there night fell and the
moon suddenly shone upon a white crescent of sand
backed by a curtain of silvery-tipped palms, their
foliage like wheels of light against a deep purple
sky. A golden pathway cut across the water and up
on the beach a row of bamboo huts were set up on
stilts. All was still. There was no breeze, just the
murmuring of the tropical night.

Faith wiped the perspiration from her brow and
then lifted her eyes to the night sky and the moon
which looked like a ripe apricot. Even the stars
looked warm, like tiny amber spearheads. But the
island held no real fascination for her. Bali was the
island of her dreams, and with a sick feeling at the
pit of her stomach, she turned away.

On the accommodation alley she stopped to listen. The men were calling, excitedly, in high-pitched voices. Faith heard the splash of a boat as it hit the water and she knew that the Captain was going ashore. The idea filled her with panic and she hurried back to her room and sat down heavily on the edge of the bed waiting for her sentence. He would come for her, she felt sure; he would have no hesitation in ordering her to leave the ship. And it was so hot. She could barely think. But what could she do? Hide away again? No, that would be ridiculous. She decided to have a shower.

Later, wrapped in a cotton kimono the Captain had left out for her use, she crept out through the office to the outer door and stood listening for a while. Captain Hilliard had not come for her. And now the Indian musicians were making their soft rhythmic music again. It floated sweetly on the night air—the gamelans this time, insistent, compelling. Now came the sound of a tiny flute. Moistening her dry lips and fighting back tears of emotion, Faith stood perfectly still, listening, and praying for a miracle. Then, because the Captain still did not come, she crept quietly back to bed where she lay tossing and turning and breaking her heart over Jeremy all over again. Three days ago she had left Singapore, and it now seemed like a hundred years. Oh, Jeremy! This time her distress went beyond tears. She could not cry; she could only lie with her eyes fixed, perfectly still. She knew that there was a chichack on the ceiling, its fat body pressed firmly to the wood, its reptile tail flagellating, but it did not worry her ...

About midnight she awoke with a start. Someone was in her room, but it was dark and she could not see who it was. She struggled up. The light snapped on and she blinked painfully across the room at Captain Hilliard. 'Come in,' she whispered, feeling rather stupid because he was already in, and it was his room. 'I knew you'd be coming for me.'

'Oh!'

He said no more, and staring at his flushed face, Faith wondered if he had been drinking. 'We've reached Labuan, then,' she said in a small resigned voice.

'Yes, we have.'

Faith sat up very straight now, staring at the old battered straw hat which the Captain was wearing and which she thought made him look like some old-style artist instead of a ship's captain. He had also discarded his jacket and the top buttons of his shirt were open. 'What is it?' she asked nervously. 'It must be late.'

Captain Hilliard roughly pushed back his battered straw hat with a strong brown hand. 'I've news for you, Miss Charteris,' he said roughly and as he advanced towards the bed. 'You *are* going to Bali.'

'Going to Bali?' Faith's heart leapt; she caught her breath and stared up at him unbelievingly.

'Yes, Miss Charteris,' he emphasised with just a hint of scorn. 'I'm afraid my island friends can't look after you. They have five children who are ill at the moment and I don't intend to add to their problem. Also, the schooner is not due for another week.' He scowled at her, then he told her abruptly, 'Plainly, I'm stuck. They don't want you—and neither do I.'

'You were going to leave me with friends?' Faith sat forward, her lips parted in astonishment, her eyes bright behind the bruising. 'You weren't just going to ...'

'Dump you beneath a banyan tree,' he finished swiftly. 'No, Miss Charteris, that is not my method. But I'd certainly made up my mind to leave you at Labuan.'

His words had no power to hurt her now. A miracle had happened! 'Oh, Captain Hilliard!' Faith's small face was alive with joy and gratitude. 'Oh, thank you a million times!' With an impulsive, youthful gesture, she reached out for his hands.

He took them and at his touch her heart fluttered like a small trapped bird. She could not draw her own hands away. The were imprisoned in his strong brown ones. She gulped down her embarrassment, moistened her suddenly dry lips.

Then she was free and the Captain was smiling in an odd sort of way and saying, 'I have something for you.' And going quickly from the room, he returned again with something in his hand. 'An orchid,' he told her stiffly. 'I brought it back from the island.'

'For me?' she stared back at him suspiciously.

'It's a dove-orchid,' he told her directly. 'The most beautiful, I think. I thought you might like it.'

'Oh, I do ... I do,' she whispered, sinking back against her pillows, the exquisite flower held gently in her hands. 'Thank you.' She raised her own dove-grey eyes and whispered, 'It's so fragile ... so lovely.'

'It is indeed, Miss Charteris.'

His voice was deep and it made Faith catch her breath. His eyes held her own and would not let her go. The room was strangely still. 'It is fragile and lovely,' he went on. 'And to a man like myself, Miss Charteris—quite dangerous.'

'Dangerous?' she questioned. She did not know what he meant, but for some reason her heart was beating very fast.

'Dangerous,' he repeated, and now a slow smile spread over his dark face and the strong mouth softened. 'Dangerous, Miss Charteris, in that its very tenderness can move a strong man like myself to emotion, to passion even.'

Faith glued her eyes to the orchid. She could not look at him now. She was breathing in fast little spurts. Then she heard him stride out of the room, saying as he went with an uncharacteristic gentleness, 'You never know, Faith, the gods may yet smile upon you. You may find your dream.'

For a long time afterwards Faith did not move. She tried desperately to think of Jeremy, but for some reason she could not. She could only think of the man who had just left her room and whose unpredictable behaviour was having a volcanic effect upon her. But she loved Jeremy! She would search the world for him!

Even so, in the darkness, heartbeat after heartbeat, Faith's thoughts were not of Jeremy but of Captain Hilliard—the great, dark giant of a man who had given her an orchid and who, for the first time, had called her Faith.

CHAPTER FOUR

FAITH had slept like a child, without stirring and with happy dreams, but now she was awake again and staring hard at the ceiling waiting for the snap back to reality. It came, she remembered everything and with a secretive little smile she gave herself a long stretch. Then she turned to the locker at the side of the bed. Yes, it was there in its small glass of water. Captain Hilliard had given her an orchid! And she was going to Bali! She was not to be put off the ship. Bali—even the name had a magical ring. Soon she would be with Jeremy.

For a few moments Faith lay still, dreaming of their meeting, dreaming herself into a fever of longing; remembering again Jeremy's kisses, his promise and her own last impulsive gesture. 'Don't make it any harder for me,' Jeremy had said, gently but firmly disentangling himself. 'We're going to England, my pet. We're going to be married. We're going to do things properly.' With a smile which she would never forget he had added, 'You're a lady, Faith. And I love you.' She remembered how she had buried her face against him and loved him a thousand times more.

Outside someone was shouting. The excited voice broke Faith's reverie. She got out of bed carefully, wondering how she would feel and found that she could walk quite well again. She went straight to the mirror and examined her face. She did not look too bad. The bruising was dying away fast and her face was no longer distorted.

She began to sing as she dressed and then someone rapped sharply at the door and she quickly fastened her dress.

It was Tan Chow, with a cup of coffee.

'All right, Tan Chow, I'll be along in ten minutes. Thank you for the coffee.'

Tan Chow bowed and smiled at her. 'Egg light boil? Toast?'

Faith nodded and waited until the door closed again before she went back to the mirror. Obviously the Captain was going to make the best of having to have her on his ship. She decided that she would be nice to him too. She wandered into the bath-room, wondering as she went how much make-up she had left. After washing, she brushed down her hair, leaving a curtain of it to hide the side of her face which was still distorted and her bruised eye. She carefully filled in her lips with a pale carnation lipstick, then she hurried back to the bedroom and instantly looked around for her sandals. But they were nowhere to be seen. For a minute or two she continued to look for them, but they had dis-appeared. She looked at the strange flower in the glass by her bed again and stood fascinated by it for a few moments. It was as alien in the Captain's bed-room as she was herself, she thought sadly—and just as desperate to get away. She gave it some fresh water and stood gazing down at the tropical flower in sympathy for a few moments. Then again she wondered what had happened to her sandals.

There was nothing else she could do, she decided, as she made her way along the deck in her bare feet. She was hungry; she wanted her breakfast. And she had been invited to the saloon. She saw Tan Chow coming along the alley and hurriedly got to the saloon door before him and pushed it open.

The men at the refectory table stopped chatting. In silence they stared up at Faith. She flushed and wriggled her toes with embarrassment, then Luke was at her side and she was being led forward and everyone was being introduced. Out of the corner of her eye she saw Captain Hilliard. He was sitting at the head of the table and he raised his bushy eyebrows and gave her a nod, but that was all. Faith flushed even harder and turned her full attention to Luke who was saying, 'This is our Third Mate, Faith, Bill Whaley.'

Faith gazed nervously into a pair of amused but indifferent blue eyes. Then she was introduced to the Second Mate, a more serious type with an intelligent, thin face and sharp eyes. He took her hand for a moment, but he did not smile.

There were two more officers who were engineers and Faith nodded briefly to them as she sat down at the heavy table next to Luke. Then the Captain sat back and all the men gave him their attention.

'Well, gentlemen,' he said deliberately. 'This is our stowaway. What do you think of her? I'd say she was a little on the lean side ...' With a flick of his hand he summoned Tan Chow. 'Give this young woman some porridge,' he said brusquely. 'And plenty.'

'Yes, Captain—at once. Plenty porridge.'

Faith could not eat her breakfast with so many inquisitive eyes examining her. At least the Captain was eating his own breakfast and ignoring her. She turned to Luke, only to find that he was getting up to leave and telling her, 'There's no need for you to hurry, Faith. Take your time.' And frowning down at her bowl, 'Try to eat something.'

The other officers eventually followed Luke one after the other, and at last Faith looked up, only to see the Captain.

'Is there something wrong with the coffee?' he asked bluntly.

'It's cold,' she retorted.

'Then don't drink it.' This time the Captain got up from his seat and went to the door. 'Tan Chow,' he shouted. 'Bring some more coffee—and don't be all day!'

Alone with the Captain, Faith squirmed in her chair. She glanced up at him again and thought how odd it was that such a bear of a man could stoop to pick an orchid. She glanced at his strong, well formed hands and then away again quickly because he had caught her eye. Then Tan Chow came silently in again and the Captain told him, 'We want two clean cups, Tan Chow. And some fresh milk.'

Faith watched the Chinese move silently across to

the large dresser which was fixed to the wall of the saloon. He brought the cups and set them out on their saucers. 'Missy pour?' he asked, backing away half stooped. 'Tan Chow fetch egg—okay?'

'Nothing more for me, thank you.' Faith frowned into space. 'I'm not hungry.' She lifted the coffee pot with a rather shaky hand.

'Here, let me do that,' the Captain said swiftly. 'We don't want any more accidents.' He looked directly into Faith's eyes for one disconcerting moment. 'Why are you shaking?' he asked her. 'I thought you were feeling much better. You should be.'

'I am,' Faith answered hotly. 'But I don't want anything to eat, that's all.'

'Then you've been crammed up in my suite too long,' he said sharply. 'I'll take you across to the island this afternoon. You need some fresh air, Miss Charteris. You look ... shall we say, a little troubled.' Leaning back to study her with cool eyes, he went on mockingly, 'Perhaps you've now decided that you would prefer to go somewhere other than Bali? Perhaps you would like me to steer yet another course, Miss Charteris.' His brow lowered and he frowned at her. 'I can see that you are in every way just as perverse as all the other female creatures I've had the misfortune to encounter.'

Faith brought down her eyelids. Her breath came quickly, in angry spurts now. Last night he had called her Faith! 'I'd like to go to the island,' she said determinedly. Frantically moistening her lips she added, 'And I promise not to be perverse.' She suddenly felt as though she was suffocating.

His hand covered his mouth as he frowned at her again. 'Haven't you got a clip or something you could put in your hair to keep it off your face?' he asked unexpectedly. 'It can't be doing it any good.'

'My face is my problem, Captain Hilliard,' she shot back hotly. 'Besides, I'm sure you would prefer not to look at it.'

'Why?' His bushy eyebrows lifted in a teasing gesture. 'Is it such a terrible face? I haven't really seen it, you know.'

'No . . . but you've made up your mind that I'm a disreputable character.'

'Did I say that?'

'You've implied it.'

He stood up and turning his face away from her for a moment he said, 'There's an old record player in my office. You might like to play it, although I don't suppose I have anything that you would really like. You're a bit young to appreciate my sort of music.'

'And silly and foolish and empty-headed,' Faith rushed on. 'How could I possibly appreciate anything?'

Captain Hilliard walked in silence to the door and then gestured to her to go ahead of him. They did not speak again until they reached his office and then he said in a more friendly tone, 'The records are in that cabinet. And don't mind Joe, the chichack. He gets a bit excited when I play something.'

'I'm not afraid of those,' Faith laughed. 'I rather like them. Besides, he just looks like a dab of paint.'

'You can be fooled by appearances, Miss Charteris. Don't forget that.'

Faith stared back at him curiously. Then she said as firmly as she could, 'I'm never fooled, Captain Hilliard. And I know why you're being kind to me.'

'Then I must congratulate you, Miss Charteris.' His bushy eyebrows rose. 'But is there any need to sound so aggressive?' His mouth almost stirred into a smile, then he said more sharply, 'Be ready at two o'clock. I'll tell Tan Chow to bring you an early lunch.' He turned to go, then turned back to her. 'I suppose,' he said soberly now and running a brown hand over his chin, 'a hard, practical man like myself could suffer from an occasional lapse ...'

Now he smiled and, almost shocked by the warmth of his smile, Faith backed a little, a new apprehension filling her. Abruptly sobered, she had become very aware of the Captain again, also of the fireworks that were suddenly exploding inside her. She stared back at him, her apprehension growing into a terrifying certainty. The exultation inside her, she knew, was aroused by the man who stood staring at her. She liked him. He excited her. She wanted him to be kind to her—more than kind! For a few traitorous moments she had forgotten her own true love, Jeremy!

Just for a moment their eyes met and held and the room was strangely still and silent, as though it too waited for some volcanic upheaval. Then he turned and was gone and Faith sat down on the rattan chair, weak with emotion, and going over and over all the pain and joy of the last moments. Her heart sank and soared again. She covered her face with her hands, fought to check the rapid beating of her heart. Then, with a great sigh, she stood up and went to switch on one of the records. Above the sound of the music she could hear the men calling, laughing and shouting. The outriggers had arrived and the loading was in process. She strained her ears again for the sound of the Captain's voice. Then, with eyes full of a painful bewilderment, she turned up the volume of the music so that she could not hear it.

Tan Chow came with her lunch at noon. She watched him set it down, but she did not speak to him until he returned to the door, then she said in a low voice, 'You're quite sure that the engineer Caithness is in Bali? You can direct me to him?'

Furtively, Tan Chow turned back. 'Tan Chow quite sure, missy,' he said in a firm voice. 'Quite sure.'

The door closed after him and Faith suddenly felt very tired. Tired of longing for Jeremy, tired of dreaming. Tears came to her eyes, then she stood up, trying hard to pull herself together, determined to fight off the attraction she felt for the Captain.

Her efforts failed when at two o'clock the Captain entered the office wearing denim trousers and an open-necked silk shirt, Caribbean style. He wore sandals and an old straw hat on the back of his dark head.

Faith began to laugh. 'You look different,' she

said self-consciously. 'I hardly recognised you.'

'Perhaps that's just as well,' he said swiftly. 'Are you ready? The boat is waiting.'

'Is Luke—I mean the First Mate—coming with us?' Faith asked.

'I'm afraid not, Miss Charteris. We're going on our own. Does that scare you?' His tone was bantering.

'Of course not!' She could not look at him. 'Why should I be scared?'

She marched ahead of him out of the door and they walked in silence along the deck to where a small group of officers were waiting to assist them into the lowered boat. It was breathlessly warm.

The island of Labuan was very beautiful; a small chip of Sarawak floating in the clear blue sea. Faith sat very still until the engine petered out and their small boat glided into shallow waters. 'It's exquisite,' she whispered, trying to ignore the explosion inside her which was caused by the touch of the Captain's arm as it brushed against hers. 'Have you been here often?'

'Yes, often. I love the place.' For the first time the dark Captain expressed some emotion. 'Labuan is Eden without its serpent. It's perfect.'

Faith bent over and trailed her fingers in the water. 'I suppose,' she said jeeringly, 'I've got to swim now.' She stared down at the smooth sand below the water. 'Although it's not very deep.'

'It's deep enough,' he told her, and quickly stripped off his trousers and with a grin stood in black trunks. Then he took off his shirt and slung it about his neck, tying the sleeves in a loose knot about his neck. 'I'll carry you,' he said. 'There's no need for you to get wet.'

With a sense of alarm Faith watched him throw out an anchor, then he clambered easily over the side and dropped into about three feet of water. 'Come on,' he called, 'let's go!'

She stretched out and put her arms about his neck, then she felt herself being carried aloft over the water. She closed her eyes and buried her face against the soft silk of the shirt about his neck, conscious of nothing else but the strong arms that held her ... conscious of no one else in the whole world but the man who held her.

'Sorry about the dress,' he said as he put her down on the shore. 'I've creased it a little, I'm afraid.' With a smile teasing about his mouth, he smoothed it down again.

But Faith swung away quickly, her face flushing hotly. 'Did you ever see anything so wonderful?' she said in a small breathless voice. 'Oh, what a lovely island!' Delight filled her eyes and she lifted her hand to shade them as she scanned the cliffs that dropped sheer into the jade sea. The sand was hot and white and Faith danced on her toes, as her eyes travelled over the gay orange foliage that coloured the slopes.

'We'll go as far as that ridge,' Captain Hilliard told her. 'We'll get some shade beneath the palm trees.'

Faith followed his gaze to a line of tall palms standing like slim feathered water birds. 'Oh, yes,' she agreed happily, 'that would be nice.'

'And you wear this,' he said, taking off his straw hat and sticking it firmly on Faith's head, 'or it won't be so very nice. You'll be in more trouble, Miss Charteris.'

'What about you?'

He had stalked on ahead and had not heard her. Faith followed him, staring as she went at his long, bronzed legs. He had a wide purposeful stride and soon she was left behind. 'Wait for me,' she called out, nervous again. 'Wait for me!' Then she suddenly screamed out. Something had shot out from the sand beneath her foot. She stared down at it in horror. It was a shaggy motorised piece of seaweed and it ran for the sea. Another small shaggy piece ran after it.

'Don't say you're scared of those little fellows?' The Captain had returned and was staring into Faith's frozen face. He held out his hand to her and it suddenly seemed natural for her to put her own into it. She forced a laugh, but she could not speak, and they walked on together until they came to some mop-headed palms, the leaves of which afforded a perfect fan-like shade.

'That's better,' Captain Hilliard said, and sank down on to the sand. He sniffed at the air. 'Can you smell copra?' he asked.

'I can smell something.'

'The copra sheds are just over the reef there,' he

told her. 'About a mile from here, there's a village. I know the doctor quite well.'

'I'm glad we're not the only people on the island.' Faith sank down beside him, but at a discreet distance. 'I was beginning to think we were.' She snapped her fingers in the air. 'The air is like silk,' she whispered dreamily. 'You can almost feel it. And the silence——' She laughed a little. 'You can hear it.'

Then they were silent and Faith lay flat on her back and thought of Jeremy. If only it had been Jeremy at her side. How wonderful it would be to lie with him on such an island ... To make love on such a dreamy island. They would eat bananas, sunbathe ... swim ... and make love again ...

'Are you all right?'

Startled from her dream, Faith craned her neck and looked up. 'I'd like you to call me Faith even if it is just for this afternoon,' she said softly. 'It makes me feel safe ... not quite so lonely.'

With a playful gesture which surprised her, he tipped the straw hat over her nose. 'All right, Faith,' he said. 'And what about cutting out the Captain for one afternoon? My name is Sebastian.'

They lay in silence for a few minutes and then Faith called, 'Sebastian!'

'Yes?'

'Nothing.' Her toes explored the white sand. 'I was just trying it out. It's rather a regal kind of name, isn't it?'

'Faith is a rather beautiful name,' he said in a

lowered voice. 'Did your mother have any special reason for giving you such a name?'

'Of course,' Faith answered him simply. 'My mother *had* faith.'

'I see ...' His voice joined the soft murmur of the sea.

'No, you don't,' she returned chokingly. 'You have to have your faith tested before you can really believe in it. Just as you have to find the fork in the road before you can decide which way to turn.'

He smiled and murmured, 'The sun is making you philosophical, Faith. You're not supposed to think in heat like this. Just relax. Think of something pleasant.'

'Is that what you're doing?'

'Of course!'

'What are you thinking about?'

'Oddly enough, a winter's day. A white Christmas back in the village where I was born. That was in the North of England a long time ago.'

Faith sat up a little, her heart beating fast. 'Do all sailors dream of home?' she asked, and her grey eyes were full of sorrow again.

'If they're English they do.'

'And if they're old?' she teased, falling back again.

'So you think I'm old?'

'I don't think anything,' she whispered, sinking into the heat again. 'I can't—I'm too hot. I don't suppose there's an ice-cream man anywhere around?' she laughed.

'I'm afraid not. An odd orang-outang, perhaps.

But I'd say you could bathe quite happily. There's a lagoon just over the top of the ridge.'

'That's a good idea,' said Faith, struggling up. 'I think I will have a swim.' She stared down at his long, dark form. 'You will stay here?'

He squinted up at her. 'Unless you'd like some help?'

'I'll be all right.' Her words faded back at him.

Faith climbed the ridge and then dropped down to the lagoon below. It was a perfect sight; blue water sheltered by a half-circle of the loveliest palms, leaning and mop-headed again, like a group of the island's most attractive layabouts. The water was still and smooth, transparent. Only the silence and calm made Faith glance warily about her. But she was alone and quickly she slipped off her dress, panties and bra, and leaving them in a little heap at the edge of the water she ran like a nymph, splashing into the blue.

It was wonderful! Floating, she dreamt of Jeremy and of how she loved him. Drifting, she thought of him. Diving and turning and splashing out on to the hot sand and back into the water again, she thought of him. She felt elated, strong again … almost happy.

She stayed too long. A voice startled her and looking up in alarm she saw that Captain Hilliard was coming over the top of the ridge and starting down to the lagoon. Horrified, she turned over and came up again, but only to stare with even more alarm at the fast approaching figure.

'Faith!'

With grace and agility she turned over in the water again.

'Faith!'

He was standing at the water's edge now. 'Please go away,' she shouted desperately.

'I told you not to stay long.' The voice was angry, but she knew instinctively that his eyes were still upon her. 'Faith! Are you listening to me?'

She dived again and this time came up with scarlet cheeks.

'If you don't come out this moment, then I'll just have to come in and get you.'

'Please go away.' She swam towards him now and raised frightened eyes. 'Please!'

For a few moments he stood very still, and then heavy lids lowered over eyes which had been full of marvelling tenderness. 'I'm going,' he called abruptly. 'I'll give you exactly five minutes.'

Floating on her back again, Faith watched his retreating back. She waited until he reached the top of the ridge and disappeared over the top, then as quickly as she could she swam to the edge of the water and waded breathlessly out. Almost at once she was dry and with a feeling of acute shyness she slipped on her dress and started back up the ridge.

'You're back at last,' Sebastian Hilliard said in a voice so brusque that it brought all Faith's fears rushing back. 'I thought you were going to stay in that pool all day.'

'I'm sorry. It was so nice.' She flopped down at his

side. 'There was no need for you to worry about me.'

'I seem to be constantly worrying about you.' Again there was aggression in his tone.

'Why?'

Faith's direct and simple enquiry made him turn and frown at her with some kind of dismay in his brown eyes.

'Have we got to get back to the ship already?'

He did not answer her, but something in his eyes started up havoc inside her. She moistened her lips and drew back from him a little.

But he reached out to touch her. 'Faith,' he whispered, and his eyes were as deep as peat now. 'Do you know how lovely you are? I've never seen a more lovely creature.' As he spoke he moved closer to her and lifted her hand to his cheek. 'You astound me ...'

Faith knew that something crazy was going to happen, yet she lay still. She lay still because she was suddenly tired of remembering, tired of hoping, of her own restlessness. Their eyes met and held in a new kind of wonder, and then Sebastian was between her and the sky. She gazed up at him through eyes full of tears. Then the vision of Jeremy was gone. She made no resistance as he leaned down and covered her lips with his own.

It was the most searing kiss Faith had ever known, and when he drew away for a moment she made a sound of protest. Then her arms crept about his neck and then he was kissing her, filling her body with uneasy awakenings, feelings that Jeremy had never once aroused. He kissed her again and again and soon nothing existed for her but his caresses, his mouth, his hard dark body. The world was forgotten until at last he thrust her from him and she lay panting on the sand. Sebastian Hilliard was like no one else! She loved him! She did *not* love Jeremy Caithness. The shock of this discovery made her sit up and turn to stare at the man who now lay flat on his back, eyeing her tenderly.

She was in his arms again and something inside her was swelling up with joy and impatience. 'Kiss me again,' she whispered, her eyes full of rapture. 'Oh, Sebastian! That was mad and crazy ... but so wonderful. You're wonderful!'

She struggled a little, and then she could not struggle any more. His kiss had become unendurable ...

Sebastian fell away and then he suddenly got to his feet.

Faith got up too. Surely he wasn't sorry? She stared up at him in a new kind of alarm. Or amused? He was! With a little cry of indignation, humiliation, anger, she turned and ran away down to the shore.

Sebastian got up and strode after her, catching her up and putting his arm firmly about her waist. 'Look,' he said with some of his old firmness, 'where lovemaking is concerned, I realise now that you need someone of your own age. But I didn't mean to insult you, Faith. Nor did I mean to alarm you.'

Insult? Alarm? Faith gulped down her dismay and then stared up at him in confusion. For a whim she had allowed this man to make love to her. She had betrayed Jeremy. The tension inside her was unbearable; she began to tremble. Alarm? She had never before known such exquisite pleasure. But a kiss meant nothing to a man like Sebastian Hilliard. And to please him for a few minutes, to entertain him, she had betrayed her own true love. She had betrayed Jeremy.

'Let's go,' Sebastian said on a deep breath, and taking her firmly by the arm now he steered her towards the water. 'Perhaps,' he said, as though to himself and with a short, bitter laugh, 'there is a serpent on Labuan after all.'

At the water's edge he swept her up into his arms and without a word waded out towards the small waiting boat. With her eyes tightly closed, she clung to him once more, and as she felt the touch of his skin a frenzy of joy broke loose inside her.

She watched in silence as he started up the engine, wondering what it would be like to be really loved by a man as magnificent as Sebastian Hilliard. What would it be like to be loved by him truly and for ever and ever? She thought about him until she felt sick with guilt, and was relieved when they reached the ship and what seemed like reality again.

The noise of the engine petered out and she stood up shakily. Sebastian reached out to squeeze her hand. 'Well,' he asked in a lowered tone, 'are you going to go on calling me Sebastian, Faith? Or do I have to put my foot on that serpent?'

Words failed her; she could not answer him. But the look in his eyes as he continued to study her made her heart skip a beat and she knew that she would never, never tell him about Jeremy. It was an unfaithful thought, she knew, but she could not help herself. Even if it was just once more, she wanted Sebastian to kiss her again; even if it was for his amusement alone—that was all that mattered in the world to her.

CHAPTER FIVE

Back in her quarters, Faith paced from chair to bed and then from bed to chair, her face very pale again. Then, on an impulse, she ran out of the room and along the accommodation alley where she climbed the ladder to the bridge deck. She scrambled on and, as she stumbled over a coil of rope, she bumped into Captain Hilliard. 'I was looking for you,' she gasped. 'I wanted to tell you that I'm ready to go back to the other cabin ...'

'You're very eager to get away from me.' He looked at her with mockery in his gaze. His eyes taunted her for a moment and then his expression grew sober. Roughly, he said, 'I kissed you and you're off like a rabbit. Is that it?' His tone was contemptuous as his eyes swept over her. 'It seems that the sea air has done you no good, Faith.'

She backed away. 'I'd prefer it if you called me Miss Charteris,' she whispered. 'And I am going back to that other cabin.'

He remained silent for a moment, gazing down at her thoughtfully. He seemed to have come to a decision suddenly and told her firmly, 'Go back to your quarters, Faith, and don't bother me at the moment. And understand this—from now on I'm not prepared to act as your nursemaid. You're quite

a woman, you know. You've proved that.' He turned
to walk away from her calling as he did so, 'Stop
taking life so seriously, Faith. Just take everything
as it comes along. Don't fight destiny—and don't
fight me.'

Slowly, with a desperate feeling inside her now,
Faith went back to the Captain's quarters and
straight to the bathroom. What was her destiny?
Was she really in love with a man who merely got
some pleasure out of taunting her? First he called
her a child, then a woman. He was kind to her, then
he was cruel. There was no one as unpredictable as
Sebastian Hilliard. And no one as wonderful! She
took a shower and then quickly wrapped Sebastian's
kimono about her. Then there was a tap on the
outside door.

This time it was Luke, and he stared at her in
surprise.

'Hello!' he said, but he was frowning. 'I thought
you'd be in hiding. The old man's in one hell of a
mood—I wonder why. An afternoon on the island
would have done me a world of good, if it had been
with you, Faith.'

'Luke, please leave me alone, if you don't mind.
I'm tired.'

'Oh, so you're both out of sorts. What happened,
Faith? Don't you think you should tell me about
it?'

'Nothing happened.' Faith tried to sound con-
vincing. 'What could happen with a man like that?'

'I don't know. He doesn't take me to his favourite

haunt. The old man always goes to Labuan alone. We think it's where he does his dreaming.'

'I can't imagine him dreaming.' Faith turned into the room and Luke followed her.

'You're quite cosy in here, aren't you?' he noted as he glanced about the office-sitting room and through the open door into the bedroom. 'It's just as well the Captain doesn't like women. Now if it had been me ...'

'Luke, please, will you stop talking rubbish! I'm tired and I want to rest.'

'Faith,' Luke moved up beside her, 'I'm honestly thinking of quitting the sea. I've been thinking a lot about it ...'

'And it's done you no good, Luke. Will you please go?'

Luke frowned. 'You're very edgy,' he said, and his voice was full of concern now. 'Faith, are you sure everything is all right? If I thought that devil...'

'Which devil, Mr Mate?'

Neither of them had heard the Captain step into the room, but they turned to him in alarm as he went on in a toneless voice, 'Mr Mate, I'd like a word with you on the bridge, if you can spare a moment?'

Faith bit her lip as she watched Luke follow Sebastian out. Dumbly she stared after them, unable to call even a faint 'goodnight'.

She sat down on the rattan chair and waited for Tan Chow to bring her some food. But she was unable to forget the events of the afternoon, and images of her encounter with Sebastian crowded upon her mind. She moved across the room, then stared in amazement at the glass on the bedside locker. Somehow, Sebastian had managed to get a fresh orchid. And this one was truly beautiful: a luminous white dove-orchid this time. As she stared at it, carefully touching the orchid's crimped petals, she felt strangely calm. She began to think about Jeremy again and her plans to follow him, find him and prove her love for him. It would not be difficult, she told herself. She would get a job first. Surely in a town crazy with tourists there would be plenty of work? She would hear things, she would eventually trace Jeremy. Then there would be the sheer rapture, their joy at being together again.

But even as she thought of the joy of her reunion with Jeremy, Sebastian Hilliard's face was lurking in her mind. She could not get rid of his image. She could not forget his kiss ... and every thought hooked on to another thought, until there was no room in her mind for Jeremy. She covered her face with her hands in an effort to blot out the picture, but Sebastian Hilliard was still there. It was almost as though he had taken control of her mind.

What was the use of fighting? Faith told herself, before she eventually fell asleep that night. Destiny would have its way, there was nothing she could do until they reached Bali. Then Sebastian Hilliard would never trouble her again.

'Breakfast over, missy. Missy sleep tight.'

Faith rubbed her eyes and sat up, startled by Tan Chow's voice. She looked around and up at Tan Chow again. 'We're moving,' she whispered.

'Yes, missy, we go now. Soon reach Bali.' He backed to the door. 'Tan Chow bring coffee.'

'Just a minute.' Faith's voice was sharp. 'You will tell me where I can find the engineer Caithness?'

Tan Chow nodded and then glanced furtively out of the half open door. 'Yes, yes, missy. Tan Chow write address on paper. Tan Chow will write.'

'How long will it take us to get there?' Faith asked quickly.

'Three days, missy. Captain say so.'

'Is the Captain about?'

'Captain busy, missy.'

'Coffee and toast, that's all, Tan Chow.'

'Good, missy. Come quick.'

Faith stayed in her bedroom until the afternoon and then she heard Sebastian come into his office and start rummaging about on his desk. She stood very still, listening, wondering if he would come in and speak to her, wondering if she should go out to him. Then she heard the drawer of the desk snap shut and retreating footsteps. He had gone—and without even looking in to see her. She turned pink with humiliation, then furiously she turned to stare at the fresh orchid again. It was hideous, she decided. It looked like a spider. It was not beautiful at all.

Faith spent the next two days in confused speculation. Luke escorted her around the decks once or twice and as cheerfully as ever. At meal-times the Captain was courteous, but formal and cold. Faith felt his eyes hard upon her now and then and in swift response she turned to look deeply into them hoping to find something quite different there. But he seemed to be unconscious of her presence. He was definitely keeping out of her way.

The evening before they reached Bali, she was surprised when Sebastian approached her. 'I'd like a word with you, Faith,' he said, entering her cabin.

'Yes, yes!' Faith's heart beat fast again. He had not forgotten her name! 'Come in, Sebastian.'

For a few moments they stood staring at each other, and Faith saw his throat work. He moistened his lips. 'I'm sorry I've been so much trouble,' she said in a small voice, but the eyes which she raised were still accusing. 'Thank you for the fresh orchid. I don't know where you could have got it.'

'I didn't get it. Perhaps it was Luke?'

Luke! Faith turned crimson this time. 'Oh,' she said, 'I see,' and she turned away from him in embarrassment.

'It's about tomorrow,' the Captain went on quickly. 'We have some officials coming on board. You'll have to see them, I'm afraid—but I expect you realise that.'

'Of course! Would *you* like my fingerprints?'

Ignoring her sarcasm, he went on, 'There'll be no bother, Faith. No trouble. You'll be in Denpasar by midday, and that's what you wanted, isn't it?'

She nodded.

'Have you friends in Denpasar?' For a moment his dark eyes were gentle and full of concern.

'I'll be perfectly all right. I can look after myself.' Faith tore her eyes away from him. 'As you said, I'm not a child. I don't need a nursemaid.'

'I said I could no longer be your nursemaid, which is a different matter altogether. You surely understood?'

'I don't understand you at all. You've ignored me since that afternoon on the island.' Faith's face was stiff with indignation. 'Just what kind of a person do you think I am?' Her eyes were full of scorn. 'I suppose every time you feel like a bit of nonsense you take a girl to your precious island?' Fury strangled her words now, her breath came in little spurts. She stared at him, hating him, loving him. How could a man come to mean so much in such a short time? Why was Sebastian Hilliard like no one else?

She turned away from him, weak again with the memory of the pleasure he had given her, pleasure which she had not known existed.

'Be ready about nine o'clock.'

She could not answer him. But she heard the door close a few moments later and she knew that he had gone and that he would not return until the next day. All this, she thought in her agony, all this because of one stolen afternoon. Even when she was married to Jeremy, she would have the pain of Sebastian Hilliard's kisses in her mind for ever.

Never would she be able to forget the fact that she had betrayed Jeremy.

At eight o'clock the following morning Tan Chow came to her cabin with a cup of tea. His manner was more furtive than usual and his voice was so low that she had to strain forward towards him to hear it. 'Is there something wrong?' she whispered, and for some reason her heart was beating very fast.

'Missy be ready in ten minutes,' Tan Chow said swiftly. 'Tan Chow go ashore for stores. Hide missy in boat.'

'You've heard from Jeremy?' Faith could barely get her breath. 'You know where he is?'

The Chinese nodded. 'Boat ready. Come quick.' He backed away as he spoke and left the room as silent as he had found it. The door closed and quickly Faith got out of bed. She was going to see Jeremy at last; within hours she would be in his arms again! Tan Chow terrified her, but she would never, never forget his kindness. And somehow ... somehow she would forget Sebastian. What was a kiss? What was a caress? There was no time for remorse or regrets. There was just Jeremy. Eventually Sebastian would sail far away over the horizon of her mind; he would be no more than a memory. She felt almost happy again.

Denpasar was thronged with tourists all enchanted by the magic of the island, despite the fact that it had not rained for weeks and was very hot and dusty. Faith went into the coffee bar where Tan

Chow had told her to wait, and pushed her way to a small single table near the counter. One of her heels was skinned through forcing on her salted sandals, so she eased the sandal off and sat with the painful foot on top of the good one. It had been dreadful getting away from the ship, but they had managed it; she had escaped. She began rummaging in her bag for some money, and it was while she was doing this that she felt that someone had their eyes hard upon her.

She raised her eyes quickly and met the cold stare of the Indonesian waitress who was standing behind the counter. Faith looked away and back again, nervously, realising that the girl meant to hold her attention. She sat back and stared at her with bewilderment, and then the girl suddenly left her post and approached her. She was large and beautiful with enormous, almost Spanish eyes, a light brown complexion and with black shining hair piled on the top of her head rather carelessly. She wore a Western mini-skirt and a near transparent blouse and as she reached Faith's table most of the other eyes in the coffee bar reached it too.

Faith stared anxiously up at the girl, wondering what she wanted.

'Tjamil wants to speak to English miss,' the girl said in an undertone. 'Tjamil at door. Please come.' Faith glanced at the door, her heart hammering fearfully now. 'I don't know any Tjamil,' she said rather sharply. 'I just want some coffee.'

'Tjamil my brother. He has message for you.

Please come.' The girl's eyes flashed impatiently.

'A message?' Faith frowned and sat back wondering 'whether she should get up and leave the bar. 'What kind of message?'

The girl bent low now and spoke in an urgent tone. 'A message from Tan Chow. Tan Chow has talked with Jer-o-mi. Come quick—please!'

Jeremy! Perhaps he was there somewhere in the coffee bar? Faith's heart turned over at the idea. Trembling, she reached down to pull on her sandal, then she quickly got up and followed the Indonesian girl.

But Jeremy was not at the door, only a small, wiry Balinese man in oil-stained jeans and a rough blue serge jacket. Faith drew back. She thought the stranger looked like some kind of tout or drifter. She did not like the way he jangled the loose change in his pocket or the way he poised on his toes as though ready to spring. Instinct made her turn away.

But already he had placed his hand on her arm. 'You Miss Faith Charteris?' The grip tightened.

Faith winced and pulled her arm away. 'Yes,' she faltered. 'I'm Faith Charteris. What do you want?'

The Balinese rubbed his hands over his slim hips and nodded. 'Tan Chow send me. He say me take missy to Sorgre, to the engineer Caithness. He pay me.'

A surge of emotion almost sent Faith tottering, but she managed to control herself. 'Sorgre?' she whispered. 'You mean Jeremy Caithness is at Sorgre?'

'Yes, yes!' The little man grew excited. 'Me take missy to engineer. Tan Chow pay well. Got car—old jeep.' Wildly now he gestured to the edge of the wide footwalk where a dilapidated jeep was parked. 'Hurry, quick!' he urged, and his whole body was alive and dancing. 'Many kilos to Sorgre.'

Faith turned to speak to the girl, but she was gone. Hesitantly she turned back. 'All right,' she agreed, 'take me to Sorgre. I expect it's a village?'

'Yes, yes, Sorgre a very fine village. The village called Heaven. That is so.'

'The village called Heaven,' Faith repeated, but unbelievingly. And suddenly her eyes were filled with sadness. How did anyone know what heaven was like, she pondered wistfully, until they had been there?

She got in the jeep and the little man gestured wildly and with some kind of wicked delight as the old vehicle leapt into life. 'Many kilos,' he shouted excitedly. 'Go quick!'

Faith sat stiffly on her seat. Suddenly she was afraid. Even the scenery frightened her. Mysterious and powerful, Bali's cluster of volcanic mountains loomed ahead, Gunung Agung's shoulders shawled by cloud. Below, the terraced rice fields shimmered and rippled and, as they climbed, the air grew moist and the foliage in the ravines more lush. Water dripped from every available cavity, spilling over every cliff edge water greedily collected from the late monsoon.

Soon the track grew worse, steeper, its edges falling away to plantations of sarak palms, small bushy trees, elephant's ear, tjempaka trees. All scented the air. Then they came to a stream where Tjamil stopped his jeep with a fearful jolt. Swinging out on to the ground, he ran to Faith's side. 'Missy get out now,' he called in a shrill high voice. 'Sorgre! See!' He lifted one thin brown arm and pointed the way. 'Across the bridge,' he explained. 'Sorgre up the hill.'

Faith dropped to the ground on shaking legs and with horror in her eyes she stared at the driver. 'Aren't you coming with me?' she gasped. 'You're surely not going to leave me?'

'All same, yes.' The Balinese grinned and bowed. 'Caithness ...' his smile was strangely mocking. 'Tuan Caithness wait only for missy.'

Protests were useless. Without a word the driver sprang back into his jeep and reversed noisily. Then, with a cry, he was off.

Faith, watching the receding jeep, felt her legs turn to rubber. Somewhere a dog howled and another answered it with a bad-tempered yap. Fear crept over Faith's skin, perspiration ran down the nape of her neck, down her back. The cloying scented air made her feel sick, dizzy.

So much for the village named Heaven! She turned towards the bridge and the dilapidated heap of clay huts which lay beyond it. A village shaded by a great cluster of bamboo leaf and palm. A village, so far as she could see, built without plan. It lay like an old deserted nest recessed into the mountain. To the west of this kampong, down a steep slope, tall palms rose from a sea of sarak bright with a flame flowering.

Faith crossed the small broken bamboo bridge and started along the muddy track that ran along to the kampong. Three brown children, nude and with sticks, appeared. They were chasing some screeching, tatty, tired-looking hens, but when they saw Faith they stopped to gape and giggle, pointing at her and talking in their own language. Faith passed on and with whoops and shrieks the children ran down to the stream, a very thin dog following them.

Further on she came to three upright boulders standing up on edge and leaning against each other. She remembered that the Balinese people were Hindu also and that the stones had been put there to keep away evil spirits. A shadow of gloom passed over her now, but she kept on walking, listening as she did so to the pound of her own heart and the rush of water coming down from the gulleys of the big mountain which backed the village.

Every time fear gripped her a picture of Sebastian Hilliard came to her mind. His image was with her when she peered around a corner and stared in amazement at a large bamboo shed. It was a shelter resting on palm posts and beneath it a number of brown-skinned women pounded rice and chatted shrilly. Benumbed, Faith watched the golden husks fall through the sieves to the ground. The women had not yet heard her approach. She made a noise in her throat and one of the younger women caught sight of her and promptly dropped her sieve. She threw up her arms in a gesture of both beauty and alarm, causing the whole company to turn and stare at Faith.

They were women of varying ages and shapes wearing their dark hair either tightly bound up or falling loosely over their shoulders. The nearest girl wore trails of love-lies-bleeding behind both her ears. The slim girls wore skirts and bright bikini tops while the elder women wore sarongs and towels bound about them instead of Western dress.

The silence grew. It was broken by a pot-bellied child who called fretfully, 'Ngurah! Come see.' Then he began to whimper and fan himself with a banana leaf. 'Ngurah!'

Ngurah appeared from behind a bamboo screen. She was an exquisitely beautiful girl with a coppery skin and enormous wary eyes. Her long black hair hung like a shawl to her shoulders and she wore a sapphire sarong and a red shiny cotton *kebaya* or blouse. When she saw Faith she stood as though spellbound, like a dark statue, her eyes still and filled with dismay. When at last she did speak Faith was shocked at the hardness in the voice of such a lovely creature.

'Speak out,' the young Balinese girl called. 'What do you want?'

The women behind Faith murmured together, clasping the magic amulets about their throats, for the Balinese–Hindu people live in a world inhabited by a multitude of spirits, some evil, some good.

Bravely Faith stepped into the shelter. In her

mind, Sebastian was at her side to give her courage. 'I have come to find the English *tuan*,' she said slowly and deliberately, for even the thought of Sebastian Hilliard gave her strength. 'English sailor, Tuan Caithness ... tall, blond ... he's here, yes?'

Faith waited, but there was no sound, no stir. Only Ngurah had caught her breath and now the dismay in her eyes had turned to real fear. Faith turned to the girl and held her eyes. 'Have you seen the *tuan*?' she asked.

The girl stared back. '*Tuan* not here,' she said too defiantly. 'Not here. What would English sailor want here?'

The women began to titter and giggle, and watching closely, Faith saw Ngurah flash them a warning glance.

'Remember my uncle Agung, the witch doctor,' Ngurah called again, but this time she addressed the gigglers, and there was a different kind of warning in her tone.

The women instantly fell silent and Ngurah turned back to Faith. 'You cannot stay here, woman,' she said, and her eyes were black with hatred now. '*Tuan* is not here.'

Faith held her ground. Instinctively she knew that the Balinese girl was hiding something. Fighting for time, she whispered, 'Could you please give me a drink? I've come from Denpasar, and I'm hot.' With a quick glance at the girl, she pleaded, 'If *Tuan* is not here, I must find someone to take me back. I will pay.'

Ngurah turned to the women with a smile. They

would find a driver. The dusky child picked up a
bamboo cane and went shrieking after a mob of
dirty little piglets which had come snorting into
the shade.

Faith began to think quickly, then she turned to
meet the sultry eyes of the Balinese girl again. 'It's
a great pity that I cannot find this man,' she said
with a sad shake of her head. 'I have a very impor-
tant message for him.' Lowering her voice, she told
the girl in whispered confidence, '*Tuan* Caithness
is in great trouble. I wish I could have helped him.
I knew him once. He was kind to me.'

'What message?'

The agitation in the girl's eyes betrayed her. Now
her face began to work, her mouth grew slack and
she was no longer sure of herself. 'What message?'
she asked, and her eyes grew sly. 'If the *tuan* passes
this way I could then give it to him.' She paused for
a moment as though making up her mind about
something, then she said swiftly, 'Stay here. Wait. I
bring you water.'

But Ngurah did not bring water, nor did she return. Faith waited until all the women had gone and
then she stepped out from the shelter and peered
down the squalid alley. Through a gap between two
windowless hovels, she caught sight of the terraced
rice fields, now gleaming gold against a brilliant
blue sky. Then she looked up and saw that the
volcanic head of the mountain Gunung Agung was
still swathed in cloud. Oppressed by the brassy heat,
she retreated into the shade and stood for a while

watching an enormous spider dangling from one of
the rafters of the shelter. Sorgre, she thought desperately, was no heaven. It was like a black sore at the
base of the mountain; she hated it. The place filled
her with fear and apprehension. But Jeremy was
here somewhere, she told herself, she felt sure of it.
That was why she could not take to her heels and
leave. She had to stay.

The place seemed dead. Then someone screamed
and a dog barked and Faith fell back with terror in
her eyes. She was a long way from Denpasar. It
would soon grow dark.

'Ngurah!' she called out. 'Ngurah!' she called
again, and came out again into the full blast of the
sun. 'Where are you?'

'I am here.' The girl appeared in front of Faith
as though by magic.

Faith stared at her. There was no sign of any re-
freshment.

'*Tuan* is not here,' Ngurah said, and her tone was
insolent now. 'You must go.'

Faith stared back into the eyes of the girl whose
confidence had for some reason returned. 'Where
have you been?' she asked levelly. 'You seem to have
forgotten the water. You said you would get me a
drink.'

Ngurah's breath came quickly, her eyes grew wide
and strangely luminous. 'You go now,' she hissed.
'Go now before the night of no moon—Ngurah says
go. Bad things happen in this village. Bad things
on the night of no moon.'

I can believe it, thought Faith, but she said, 'Would you then please find someone to drive me back? There must be someone with a truck.'

'You go quick?' The girl was smiling now. 'I send Rami—he has lorry.'

'I'll wait down by the bridge,' Faith said as she turned to go. 'Send Rami quick.'

There was something wrong, Faith thought as she made her slow way back along a wide rut in the alley and then down the slope to where the children were still playing at the edge of the stream. Why had Ngurah refused to give her a drink? Had she been told by someone not to do so? Disconsolately now, Faith turned back to glance once more at the mysterious village, then she picked up her heels and decided that there was nothing she could do but go.

There were a dozen or more naked children playing by the edge of the stream; a grubby bunch of youngsters who seemed, nevertheless, to be enjoying themselves. Two thin mongrels yapped excitedly, enticing them on. Faith paused to stare at the children and, seeing her, they stared back at her curiously.

Suddenly she noticed that one of the small boys was wearing a cap—*a sailor's peaked cap*. It was tilted jauntily on the back of his dark head: a white, peaked, officer's cap. With a cry, Faith ran back to the child.

The moment she reached him she saw his small hand reach for his amulet, a silver box which hung about his frail neck. His black eyes were riveted upon her.

'Boy,' she whispered breathlessly, 'who gave you that cap?'

The small boy backed into the water, splashing water as he went, but saying nothing.

'Boy!' Faith followed him to the water's edge. 'Tell me who gave you that cap.' She dived into her bag. 'I'll give you chocolate.' She held up a bar. 'Come back, please. Chocolate!'

The child returned slowly, suspiciously and with the rest of the tribe greedily behind him, their eyes wide and curious. Faith touched the cap. 'Who gave it to you?' she whispered.

Still the child did not understand. But with a whoop of delight he snatched the chocolate from Faith's hand and went hurtling off towards the village, the other children running wildly after him.

Faith watched him go. Her intuition had not deceived her. Tan Chow had not deceived her. Jeremy was somewhere in the village—and for some reason the villagers were hiding him. For some reason, not even a child would give him away.

What could she do? She could not leave him. Once again the old yearning for Jeremy enveloped her and for a few moments she stood lost in thought. Then the sound of a lorry starting up somewhere reminded her that she was about to be taken back to Denpasar.

But she could not leave now. Somewhere amidst

the dark jumble of huts Jeremy was in hiding. She was going back; she could not leave him. She glanced up. The great mountain behind the village was festooned with cloud, but the sun was at its height and it was siesta time. The villagers would be sleeping. Making her mind up quickly, Faith darted back up the slope and quickly made her way back along the muddy lane. The sound of the lorry starting up again alarmed her and she quickly backed into something that looked as though it had once been a garden. Listening to the lorry, she took refuge behind a profusion of thick bushes heavy with waxy gardenias and thick pink blossom.

The man driving the lorry would be looking all over for her. She bent down, lowered her head ... and went rigid with shock. Not far from her feet lay the husk of a dead snake recently scavenged by white ants, some of the ants were still lingering. She glanced away. She heard the lorry lumbering by, skidding down the lane, noisily changing gear as it started down the bank to the bridge.

Creeping out of the garden, she made her way along an even more narrow and more muddy alley. The village was eerily silent, the children mysteriously spirited away. It was all so remote, worlds apart from tourist Bali.

Faith stiffened and stopped again, straining her ears this time. Somewhere a girl was laughing, low and provocatively. The laughter drifted out from one of the windowless hovels. Faith backed again into a dim doorway and waited, holding her breath.

Then she flitted across the alley and startled some fighting cocks asleep in their basket. The next dwelling appeared to be sitting on a spring, for it was sunk in mud and water. A rubbish dump stood at the door and Faith thought it must have been vacated recently.

She peered in the doorway and to her astonishment saw two saronged figures lying asleep on some old bamboo matting which had been strewn over the floor. Like a ghost she passed on, then turned into yet another slippery passage, then only a few yards further ahead she saw a house which was a little more prepossessing. It was higher than the rest and it had a red-tiled roof; the walls were thatched. It had a gateway too, a double-leaved door. Just outside the doors lay all kinds of pieces of carving and odd stones, some of which were wrapped in banana leaves. These, Faith knew, were offerings to the spirits, bribes to keep evil ones away.

She stood still for a moment, trying to get her bearings, but it was impossible. She was lost in the maze of the kampong, she had no idea where she was. Then she heard a girl laugh again, teasingly. She doubled up and listened carefully, then she gently eased open the leaved doors and after tiptoeing a few feet, peered inside what seemed to be a very large room. At one end of the room two mosquito nets lay like crumpled clouds upon some coconut matting. There was a small table with an oil lamp standing upon it and two rattan chairs.

Faith took one more step and peered around a woven leaf screen—and what she saw then tore the breath from her body.

Ngurah, the beautiful sensuous Balinese girl, lay upon a small bed of slats and at her side, kneeling on the floor, bending over her, was the figure of a man. He was young and lithe, fair and handsome, his skin well bronzed, and Faith knew in one agonized moment that it was Jeremy who was down on his knees making passionate love to the girl who gazed up at him with focused, luminous eyes, lips parted in joyous assent.

Like a ghost, Faith backed away, her own lips trembling, her limbs shaking. Blindly, she stumbled and cried out, and in a moment the figure on the floor was up and turning to glare at her through eyes glazed with lovemaking and strong wine.

'Jeremy!' Faith whimpered in recognition. 'Oh, Jeremy!'

CHAPTER SIX

'So you were fool enough to follow me!'

Faith opened her eyes and almost passed out again at the sound of Jeremy's harsh words. Then the horror of everything filtered back into her brain and she fought giddily to keep her senses. Jeremy was standing over her, but not the Jeremy she had known in Singapore, not the Jeremy with whom she had been in love. There was a leer on this man's thin face and she shuddered at the expression in his washed-out blue eyes. He was dirty and unkempt, the muscles of his face slack. Faith stepped instinctively backwards and flinched as she banged her head on a bamboo partition. She fell to the floor, dazed. Then slowly her eyes began to focus again and she saw the girl, Ngurah, was still there.

Deeply shocked, Faith bowed her head again. Completely shattered, she could not look at the man who had so cruelly deceived her. The small rattan table in the centre of the room came into focus and she kept her eyes hard upon it. Even her pride could not insulate her against the shock of finding in such a situation the man she had trusted and loved completely. She had travelled miles only to find him in a hovel making love to another girl, and now she realised only too well that Jeremy Caithness was one of the men the police were seeking.

'So you've managed to put the police on my trail? Now aren't you a clever girl?' His face twisted and his mouth grew cruel. 'And I suppose you've come to tell me how much you love me.'

For the first time Faith raised her eyes to the dirty, unshaven man who mocked her. She could see in one glance that he had gone native. She knew too that he had been involved in a Chinese opium syndicate. It was all written in his eyes. He was guilty; he had been smuggling opium. It was the last disgrace for a white man and Jeremy had succumbed to it. She tore her eyes away from him again, praying that it was all some dreadful nightmare; that it was not true.

But it was. Faith watched the Balinese girl come forward and with a wave of repulsion saw in the manner the girl swayed sinuously against Jeremy exactly what had been going on. She turned away from the girl's hot, possessive eyes as her own filled with angry tears.

'So you don't like Ngurah?'

Again Jeremy's words were mocking, full of jest—and hatred too. Faith covered her face with her hands for a moment, but she heard him taunt, 'Well, I don't think Ngurah cares too much for you either, Faith.'

'She must go. She must go,' the Balinese girl cut in. '*Tuan* must send this woman away. She make big trouble.'

'We won't be so hasty, my dark beauty,' Jeremy said, and suddenly grabbed Faith's arm and pulled her roughly to her feet. His eyes were menacingly close to hers. 'Now,' he said through gritted teeth, 'just who told you to follow me here? Who told you to come to Bali?'

Faith struggled free, but Jeremy caught her arm again and this time she could not escape from the cruel fingers which probed her soft flesh. 'Speak out,' he demanded. 'Who told you that I'd gone to Bali?'

Praying for courage, Faith faced the red-rimmed eyes. Her throat was full, tears gushed to her eyes again. This was the man for whom she had suffered humiliation and discomfort. She whispered desperately, 'Jeremy, you're ill. You don't realise it, but you're ill.'

'Ill?' His laugh was ruthless, his expression crude as he smiled at the dark girl by his side. 'Ngurah thinks I'm fit enough. And believe me,' he taunted her, 'Ngurah is no pale white dove.'

'*Tuan*, the white girl must go. She must go,' Ngurah began to protest again. 'Send her away!'

'Where, you fool?' This time Jeremy's fury was unleashed upon the native girl. 'Back to Bali? Back to tell the police where I am, if they haven't already followed her here?'

'*Tuan!*' The girl's voice was soft. 'Ngurah will honour and serve.'

Jeremy relaxed his grasp on Faith and smiled at the native girl. 'Of course you will, my gentle tigress. But we do have a problem.'

'Trouble?' Ngurah's eyes flashed. 'Agung, my uncle, has much black magic. He get rid of trouble.' With a slow smile she fixed her eyes upon Faith. 'He will deal with this girl, *Tuan* Jeremy.'

Jeremy's eyes gleamed with malice. 'Agung certainly is a clever devil.' He grinned and looked right into Faith's eyes. 'I think you should meet him, Faith,' he said significantly. 'Yes, we must arrange it.'

Ngurah laughed. 'Yes, *Tuan*, this white girl must meet Agung from the mountain. He is in Sorgre this very day. Is it not the night of no moon?'

His eyes still upon Faith, Jeremy slipped his hand along the back of the native girl's neck, pushing back her blouse and lifting her long dusky hair to expose one of her satin shoulders. Ngurah purred with pleasure. 'The *tuan* will protect Ngurah for ever?'

With a sudden jerk Jeremy sent the girl sprawling, then he grabbed Faith's arm again. 'Who put you on to my trail?' he demanded in a staccato voice. 'You haven't told me yet, and I want to know.'

Faith bit her lip, then she gasped, 'Tan Chow. It was Tan Chow, Jeremy.'

'The devil! The cunning old devil!' His voice held a snarl of hatred. 'So you were fool enough to fall into his trap.' His voice grew sneering now and he turned to Ngurah again. 'Ngurah,' he said in an almost sinister tone, 'would you believe that this white milksop actually thought I wanted to marry her? She came here because she loved me so much. She would like me to be tethered to her for ever and ever.'

Giggling again, Ngurah ran to his side, pressed

her slim hip against his, raised one hand to his neck.

'Could you ever look like Ngurah?' he asked Faith contemptuously. 'You imbecile! I used you and your bungalow. You were both very useful.' He laughed hatefully. 'Words are feeble, my very English Faith Charteris. Words don't mean a thing. Look at Ngurah, she doesn't need to speak at all.' Turning to the native girl, he changed his tone and said quickly, 'Keep this white girl here, Ngurah. Keep her well hidden.' He pulled his mouth and then pursed it significantly. 'She never came to Sorgre. You understand?'

The girl nodded. 'You must go?'

'For a short time. But I will come back and make Ngurah a rich woman.'

'*Tuan* will be rich?'

Jeremy's mouth pulled mockingly as he turned to Faith again. 'Rich enough perhaps for two wives,' he taunted. He gave another harsh laugh as he glanced at Faith. 'Well, isn't that what you came here for? You want to be my wife, don't you, Faith?' and with another diabolical leer, 'you love me, don't you?'

The Balinese girl moved back into the shadows as Jeremy spoke, but the moment he had gone her mood changed. She turned upon Faith, her lustrous eyes full of fear and fury. 'I warned you,' she cried out, overcome by jealous fears now. 'This is the night of no moon. Many bad things happen. Many people cry out.'

Faith met the girl's troubled eyes. 'The *tuan* will

deceive you as he has deceived me,' she said slowly. 'Believe me.'

'You lie!' Ngurah raised her hands as though to strike, but for some reason they dropped to her slim hips again. 'You lie,' she said more calmly. 'And a lie is a fault. Agung's magic will get through—you will see. Ngurah does not lie. Ngurah has no fault.'

Faith did not answer the girl. What was the use? A deathly shadow had fallen upon her own beautiful past; it was over. It would surely fall upon the Balinese girl too, for she could see that the girl loved Jeremy deeply. For a moment Faith's heart welled with compassion for the simple native girl. As for her threats, they just made her smile. You had to believe in black magic before it could do anything to you, and she did not. But her throat was aching and she still felt faint, so she asked, 'I'd be grateful if you would get me a drink of water, please.'

The girl hesitated, and then a strange smile flickered across her face. 'The white girl is thirsty. Her throat is rough? Good! She must thirst.'

Shakily, Faith reached for her bag. 'If you get me some water I will give you some perfume,' she whispered. 'The *tuan* loves perfume. All white men love perfume.' She rummaged in her bag and then held up the tiny bottle. 'Look,' she said, opening the bottle and holding it forward. 'Smell.'

The dark girl sniffed the air and then snatched the bottle from Faith. 'I will get water,' she said as she sniffed at the perfume again. 'Yes, Ngurah will get water.'

Alone, Faith found herself thinking of Sebastian Hilliard. She thought about him as she sat in the stuffy hut as perspiration ran down the back of her neck, until her hair lay limp and heavy. She was in a sad plight, she knew, but she was not completely lost. Oddly enough, she did not want the police to find her in Sorgre. She realised now how dangerous it would be to be connected in any way to such a man as Jeremy Caithness. He had used both her and the bungalow for illegal purposes, and the smuggling of opium was the lowest form of crime. It called for international police action. Faith bit down her lip in an endeavour to stem tears of self-pity at the thought. She had been a romantic, trusting little fool! If only Sebastian had dropped her at Labuan, if only she had never come here at all. If only Sebastian were here and able to help her out of this horrible mess!

Ngurah returned and offered Faith an old chipped cup full of water. Faith held it to her lips and drank greedily. She ran her moistened tongue over her lips and then sank back against the wall. 'Thank you,' she whispered. 'That was good.'

Ngurah smiled suddenly and approached with some new kind of delight and confidence. 'White girl go now,' she said swiftly, and glancing at the leaved door. 'Ngurah tell *tuan* that bad spirits carried white girl away.'

Faith raised her eyes to the girl. So Ngurah also

had a kind heart? Or did she love so desperately?
She felt even more sorry for her dusky sister. But she
shook her head and pointed to the door. 'It will be
dark soon,' she said.

'You will not go?' The girl's face sobered.

'Out into the night? Out into the night of no
moon? No.'

Ngurah's lips tightened defiantly. 'Then I must
speak to Agung,' she said, and the fire was back in
her eyes.

Faith thought quickly. Night had almost fallen.
There would be no moon. It would be impossible
for her to find her way down the mountain to Denpasar. It was too far and the slimy track ran for
miles through dense salak-palms, thick bushes, over
which sugar cane, coconut and vast breadfruit trees
spread their furling tops. A kind of a mini-jungle
clothed the hills and ran side by side to the terraced
rice fields. But it was not the mystery that cloaked
these forests or the demons who were supposed to
lurk in the banyan trees that made up Faith's mind.
It was the fact that the air had grown quite chill and
that her heel was so badly skinned that she knew
she could not get very far. Strangely enough, she was
not afraid. She knew Jeremy would be far away
and in a new hiding place by nightfall—perhaps
even with another native girl. She looked up at
Ngurah and said softly, 'Well, what are you going
to do with me?'

Ngurah did not answer; she had thoughts of her
own.

'You need not concern yourself,' Faith went on. 'I

will stay here until the sun rises, then I will go. But I'm warning you, Ngurah, you will be deceived. The *tuan* is a wicked man. He does not love you.'

This time Ngurah's proud head shot back and her lips curled. 'You speak lie!' she screamed. 'White girl bring devil, much unhappiness for Ngurah.' With rolling eyes and swaying hips the outraged girl backed to the door. 'This is the night of no moon,' she reminded Faith, her fury whipping up again. 'Agung is full of black magic.'

'His black magic cannot hurt me, Ngurah,' Faith returned in a weary voice. 'I have no fear. He cannot touch me.'

For a few moments the native girl stood trembling in the doorway, her face working with rage. 'Agung sent my brother's wife away,' she shouted suddenly. 'She grew thin and no good. Agung knew my brother did not want her.' Her voice rose tremulously as she stepped back into the room and glared down at Faith. 'I will bring Agung to you,' she cried out. 'Ngurah does not want *you*!'

As the darkness grew, Faith lay as though at the bottom of a pit. Nothing stirred; there was no sound, but she sat stiffly, bolt upright and alert, listening for any suggestion of movement in her dark prison. With pain she had thought of Jeremy for some long time, then for even longer she had thought of Sebastian, comforted herself with the memory of his caresses, his kiss.

Beyond the door of the hut someone screamed into the night and Faith backed even harder against the wall, fighting her fear once again with the memory of the afternoon she had spent on the island with Sebastian. Labuan! Now Labuan was the island of her dreams.

A girl's scream came again and now a cold fear crept up Faith's spine and held her at grips. Could Agung's black magic really work? What was happening outside? Her flesh crept, then the screaming stopped and now a low chant sounded monotonously on the thick night air. It was the voice of an old man praying; an indistinct and eerie lament which Faith strained her ears to hear above the loud beat of her own heart. She listened hard and missed the light footfall of Ngurah and those of her uncle Agung who was returning with her.

It was the amber glow from the oil lamp which Ngurah held aloft which first caught Faith's attention. Then she saw the shadow of the old man, and the sight of it snatched the breath from her body.

Agung came forward on soundless bare feet. He was a shrunken old man and the front of his bony bullet head was shaven; he wore a towel about his waist and in his hand he carried a joss-stick. As he came closer, Faith saw the blue bulging veins that tattooed his long skinny arms and legs. Then the flame from Ngurah's lamp caught Agung's strangely bright, starting eyes and Faith struggled to her feet.

'This is the woman,' Ngurah cried impatiently. Her scarlet blouse caught also in the flaming light made her look like some gigantic firefly. 'This is the woman who has come to destroy Ngurah's happiness!'

The old man stepped even closer and peered hard into Faith's frightened eyes. She shuddered violently and jerked back in horror as two more bright eyes glinted over the man's bony shoulder. A monkey, as old as the head-man himself, was clinging to his withered back, its eyes glinting cunningly bright in the light. Then someone screamed again in the lonely stillness of the kampong and the old man smiled, his pointed, atrophied tongue quivering like a snake between hard black gums.

Ngurah spoke confidently. 'You will help me, Agung?'

The old man muttered something in his own language.

Faith backed away, her body taut with fear now. 'You can't touch me!' she shouted. 'I don't believe in your magic. I have a God who protects me.'

A claw-like hand reached out and fastened itself upon her arm and Faith felt her strength drain from her. She fought to remind herself that there was no such thing as black magic, that the people before her were like children groping in the dark. Don't jeer, she told herself. Keep silent. Let them think that their magic is having some effect.

She swayed on her feet; despite her reasonings, disgust overwhelmed her. Close contact with the sinister old man terrified and repelled her. And now Ngurah's spicy breath was hard upon her too, and coming in fast, excited spurts. The native girl's eyes glittered with triumph.

'This white woman will be dreadfully plagued,'

Agung began in a low chant. 'She shall be weighted to the ground. She will become useless, like a husk. The white woman's spirit will die.'

Even the monkey reacted to the uncanny atmosphere, screeching in unearthly fashion and then falling silent again. In the still darkness of the night outside, in the obscurity of the kampong, another voice rose to take up the chant ... 'The white woman will become as a husk ...'

Faith felt her knees sag, her legs go weak; she sank to the ground. Only her heart leapt in fear. She did not believe in black magic, but she had a ghastly pain in her stomach. She doubled up, moaned. The pain got worse and her fear grew with it. She did not believe in black magic, she kept on telling herself.

As suddenly as they had come, Ngurah and Agung were gone and Faith was left alone; alone with the strange pain and the darkness. She was afraid, perspiration soaked her dress, her hair, the palms of her hands and her face. And with each moment the pain grew more severe. It came in merciless, agonizing waves and she felt as if knives tore at her stomach. By midnight she was unaware of her surroundings, conscious only of a cocoon of pain. She called out weakly from time to time, and then with a scream as though she was tormented. The fever attacked her mind and her body. She writhed on the hard floor, flung out her arms in a wild endeavour to find something at which to clutch. She hated all men! She hated Jeremy Caithness! She hated Luke! She hated Sebastian Hilliard, because she loved him and he was not there to save her. They had all steered her towards the evil day.

It was dawn when Ngurah came running to peer through the door again, and when the girl saw Faith, she stopped in her tracks and then backed a little, turning for a moment to look furtively behind her. The dirty, dishevelled heap on the floor was certainly no threat to her now. But she did not wish upon herself the wrath of her English *tuan*. She did not want the white girl to die. As though possessed herself, Ngurah suddenly rushed away again. A few minutes later she returned, this time carrying a cheap beaker full of water.

Faith reached weakly out to the legs of the rattan table and clung to them as Ngurah bent down and held the beaker to her lips. Then she fell back again and this time lay motionless, her small face like a death-mask.

Ngurah's throat worked; she stood up, then she backed away again, real terror in her enormous eyes now. Her lips began to quiver and when she reached the doorway she turned and ran with a great, choking cry of alarm. 'Agung! Agung!' she called hysterically. 'The white girl is dead! You have killed the white girl!'

Dead? A violent shudder told Faith that she was not. But the dreadful word plunged into her exhausted mind and set her thoughts in motion again. Could she be dying? Was this really the last straining effort of her poor tormented body? No, it could not be. No! In an act of desperation she dragged up her knees and rocked herself until the pain in her stomach subsided again. Then, utterly spent, she lay back against the hard uneven walls of the room. She would not die; she refused to die. She was only twenty.

Tears mingled with the mud and grime on her face and as she sank lower, Faith thought of Sebastian Hilliard once more. He had been so strong; if only he could send her a little of his strength to help her now! She began to cry softly and then for a while she grew strangely calm. Somehow, she told herself, she had to get away from Sorgre, from Agung. If it meant that she had to crawl away on her hands and knees she still had to go. She had to get away, far away from the devil Agung. For he had surely filled her with something as evil as himself!

But she was too late. She fell back again at the sound of footsteps. She was lost; they were coming nearer, closer ... In her last moment of dread fear she thought of Sebastian Hilliard. She closed her eyes and pretended that she was in his arms again. She thought of her gentle giant and with all the strength that was left in her body she called out, 'Sebastian! Sebastian!'

As she lay there, her energy spent, a brilliant ray of sun stabbed her eyes when the door opened. Like a wounded animal she turned away as though to shut out the world that had treated her so cruelly. Crouched on the dirt floor, she cowered and whimpered.

Then strong arms reached out and held her tight. Someone raised her up and cradled her to him. In a flash she knew that Sebastian had heard her calling and that he had come to her. She raised her trembling arms to his neck and buried her face against his throat. 'Sebastian,' she whispered brokenly, 'Sebastian, please don't leave me here. Please take me with you.'

CHAPTER SEVEN

FAITH opened her eyes and then closed them wearily again. Where was she now? At once her pulse was drumming in her ears. In that instant of awareness the glare from the light had been stunning. She realised that she was no longer in Ngurah's terrible hut.

But where was she? She felt weak, exhausted and there was a strange little twinge in her stomach. Then, quite suddenly, memory returned and the fear was back; she remembered the pain she had suffered and she held her breath. Agung, the repulsive dealer in black magic, had brought her close to death and miraculously Sebastian had saved her. But had Sebastian been in time to protect her from Agung's evil? She was shivering and dizzy again and her thoughts seemed confused with all the shocks she had suffered. Jeremy had both deceived her and betrayed her. He had murdered all hope and then left her in a dank Balinese kampong to face the prospect of death. In her agony she had conjured up a vision of Sebastian.

'Sebastian!' The name fluttered from her lips.

'Lie still, Faith. Don't struggle.'

The voice was familiar, commanding, and yet it brought a faint smile to Faith's lips. She tried to

raise her hand and smiled again as a strong hand
firmly put it beneath the rugs again. 'Sebastian ...'
she murmured.

'You're going to be all right, Faith. You're suffering from shock, that's all. Be a good girl now. Close
your eyes, get some sleep.'

'They were dreadful ... dreadful people ...'
Faith's voice faded out again.

'The natives are simple people with their own
beliefs and customs, Faith. Caithness is the devil—
a white devil!'

'Yes, yes, I know.' Faith struggled to free her hand
again. 'Sebastian,' she asked dreamily, 'did you hear
me calling to you? I did, you know ...' she fingered
the edge of the rug and once again he gently put her
hand below the covers again. 'Thank you,' she whispered. 'Oh, thank you, Sebastian.' Dreamily she repeated his name again. 'Sebastian ...'

She slept again and when she awakened three
hours later she sat up straight away. Sebastian was
still there and she said at once, 'Tell me I've been
dreaming?' Her eyes were full of entreaty. 'I must
have been! Oh, I've had the most frightful nightmare.'

'No, Faith, it was real enough. You haven't been
dreaming. You went to Sorgre.'

'But where am I now?' Faith opened her eyes
wide and struggled up higher in the bed.

'I'm afraid you're back in my bed,' Sebastian told
her with a short laugh, and his eyes met hers.

'Back on the *English Rose*?' It all came back again

and with dismay in her eyes she turned her face into the pillow. 'Is there something terribly wrong with me?' she asked shakily.

'Of course not. You had a nasty fright, that's all. And your imagination probably had a lot to do with it. You've had a nasty attack of colic. That was the cause of all the pain, not Agung's black magic.'

'Did you see him?' Faith peered up again, horror in her wide eyes now. 'Did you see that girl?'

'I saw them all,' Sebastian told her. 'And you must forget about them now. I like the Balinese natives— I find them fascinating.' He took a deep breath and said brusquely, 'As I said, Caithness was the only devil in that kampong.'

At the thought of Jeremy, Faith covered her face with her hands and it took her all her power not to cry. 'Well,' she said, looking up at Sebastian again, 'you can drop me off anywhere now. It doesn't really matter any more.' She sobbed and then asked, 'Sebastian, how did you know where to find me?'

'I'm not telepathic, Faith,' he said, and a slow smile softened his face. 'Actually, the Balinese police got in touch with me.'

'Then they're on to Jeremy?'

'Yes.' His voice was crisp. 'I'm afraid you'll have to write your precious Jeremy off as a bitter experience.' He laughed, but mirthlessly, and turning away added, 'I suggest you take our clown of a First Mate more seriously. He certainly has your good at heart. He was quite ready to murder Tan Chow, but fortunately the police collected our Chinese.'

'Did Tan Chow tell the police about me?' Faith

was shivering again, but with alarm this time. 'Do they know I'm on board your ship?'

'He told them that I had a woman on board,' Sebastian said too sharply. 'And I'm afraid I had to bluff my way out of that situation. I told the authorities that the Chinese was right and that I had a woman on board ... one I knew intimately.' As he spoke he turned to frown at her.

'Intimately?' She shrank back a little.

'Yes, intimately.' He gave a harsh laugh. 'I told them you were my wife.'

'Wife?' Faith blinked at him.

'Does the idea offend you so much?' Again he smiled. 'I'm growing quite used to you. And damn it all, I should—you never seem to be out of my bed!'

The memory of his kiss came rushing back; Faith could not speak. In confusion she shook her head a little. His wife!

'If you stay in my bed, you'll stay out of the hands of the police,' he told her roughly. 'But don't imagine you're ill. The doctor has seen you and all you need is warmth and sleep. As I've told you, Faith, I'm the Captain of this ship and not a nursemaid. And as it happens we're on the move now. We're far away from Bali.'

Far away? But where were they going now? She watched him stride from the room and go back into his office, the door closing between them. Perspiration had gathered on her eyelids and her pillow felt damp. She had been so cold and now she was so hot. She pushed back the bedclothes, then stared down

at herself with alarm. She was completely naked.
Everything had been taken out of her hands—even
her clothes!

Later that night, about midnight, Faith stirred
again. She felt much better. She remembered everything but with calmness and a sense of security.
Sebastian Hilliard had saved her; saved her from
Jeremy, saved her from Agung. Finally, he had even
saved her from the police who no doubt would have
wanted to question her. She drew a deep breath as a
new shyness rushed to colour her neck and flood her
face. She felt breathless, full of a new elation. She
was in Sebastian's bed and this time supposedly as
his wife. The idea made her heart beat faster.

She heard a sound as the door opened and she saw
Sebastian's magnificent form and strong head sil-
houetted against the lamplight from his office. She
watched him come quietly into the room, half closing the door behind him, and something inside her
made her panic suddenly.

'What do you want?' she asked over a lump in her
throat.

'Faith?'

The tone of his voice made her heart beat all the
faster. He had reached the bedside, she could hear
his fast breathing. To her alarm he made no attempt
to switch on the bedside lamp. He reached out to
touch her wrist and she drew back instantly, trembling violently.

'Faith!' His voice was sharp now, impatient.
'You're not afraid of *me*?' He tried to catch her

hand again but found that she had curled her fingers into a tight fist. In the darkness they listened to each other's breathing and then, soundlessly, Faith was pleading with her fingertips ...

The bedside lamp snapped on and she fell back, blinking up at him in embarrassment and dismay.

Sebastian was gazing at her. 'I don't suppose I really needed to take your pulse. You look all right to me.' He threw something on to the bed. 'My kimono,' he said, eyeing Faith strangely. 'You'll be needing it. I'm sorry about your dress and those other bits and pieces. They were pretty well wrecked.'

'I understand.' What a fool she was! What an idiotic fool! It was her nerves. She looked up at him, wanting to tell him so, but shrank again at the expression of contempt in his dark eyes.

'You understand very little, Miss Faith Charteris,' he said slowly and deliberately. 'You're a very foolish girl. And believe me, had it been anyone else who had questioned my integrity, they would have had to do some explaining. I was told to check your pulse rate and I had hoped to do it without awakening you. Believe me, you've nothing to fear from me.' He gave a bitter laugh that made Faith cringe, and threw at her, 'You can rest assured I'm not interested in sickly children.' He laughed again mockingly.

'Where are we sailing to?' she asked in a small contrite voice. 'I'd like to know.' Her breath caught in her throat. 'And I didn't think ...'

'I'm glad,' he shot back. 'Because every time you

do, it seems to land you in trouble. We happen to be going to England—and when we get there, I'll be more than glad to hand you over to the First Mate.'

The light snapped off again and Faith lay curled up in bed, trying desperately to comfort herself, but it was impossible. Sebastian Hilliard had put himself out to help her and she had insulted him for his pains. How could she explain, tell him of her sudden fear and distrust of men? How could she apologise? Words were so feeble. And why did she now love Sebastian so much? If only, like so many girls of her own age, she could be capable of happy abandon, content with the kind of loving her friend back in Singapore had raved about. 'A different fellow every week and a miracle every month'—that was the sophistication her friend talked about.

But no, she knew what she wanted now without a doubt. She wanted Sebastian Hilliard; she wanted to love him intimately, for ever and ever, until death. And all she could do was insult him. She turned onto her back and stared into the darkness. Yes, she knew now what she wanted and who she wanted. Yet the moment they reached England she knew that she would never see him again. What was a kiss, a caress on a lonely island, to a man like Captain Hilliard? He was not the kind of man to be made slave to any unexpected caprice. In any case, he thought she was foolish.

'Oh, there you are, Faith!'
It was Luke who bounded up the steel steps from

the accommodation alley to the deck, where Faith was standing some weeks later.

'You're looking very brown and bonny,' he told her, and his eyes were bright with admiration as he smoothed her cheek with the back of his slim hand. 'All the bumps and bruises gone.' He turned to glance away, telling her, 'But we're sailing into cold waters now. We'll soon be in England, Faith, and there'll be little sunshine there.'

Faith leant against the rails and made no comment. Her spirits were low.

'Faith—what's wrong?' Luke slipped an arm about her waist. 'Don't tell me you're still in the dumps. I thought I'd cured all that!'

Faith tried to smile, but her gaze never left the infinitely spacious sea. She seemed quite unaware of his arm around her, and eventually Luke eased it away and gripped the rails himself.

'Why do you worry yourself about the old man?' he said in a lowered tone and straight to the point. 'I've told you, Faith, the Captain doesn't hanker after women.'

'Oh, it's not that,' Faith said, flushing and wishing that the mention of the Captain did not affect her so strangely. 'He's not even polite. I don't expect him to hanker after me, Luke. You'd think he would have a few minutes to speak to me now and again. He makes me feel uncomfortable. I just wish I had the money to pay him for my passage.'

'Are you sure that's what he makes you feel, Faith?' Again Luke was direct. 'If you're in love with him, then I'm sorry for you.'

Faith made no reply and after a short silence he said, 'In a couple of days you'll be seeing those cold white cliffs.'

'Yes, you've often told me about them.' She raised a smile. 'I may yet see a white Christmas!'

'You will. I'll make sure you have a good time, Faith, if you'll let me stick around. I'd like to look after you in England. No strings either, I promise!'

'Won't you be sailing off again soon?'

'No,' Luke went on eagerly, 'we're going into dry dock—the old tub's due for a scrape. I'll have some leave. We'll have fun.'

Faith gave Luke another smile, but her thoughts were far away. Surely Sebastian would not walk off the ship without first coming to see her? Would he leave her without even a word of farewell?

'My folks have a nice little place,' Luke was going on, carried away now by thought of leave. 'They'll put you up, Faith. I'll give them a ring the moment we dock.'

'That's kind of you, Luke,' she whispered distantly and she reached out to touch his hand affectionately. 'You're always kind.'

'Who wouldn't be kind to you?' he murmured back, but now he was frowning out to sea. 'Even the old man was kind to you in his way. I'm sure he doesn't realise that he's offending you. He doesn't usually bother with women, but I must say he was concerned about you. You should have seen his face when we got you safely back to the ship! I've never seen the man so worked up.'

Faith took a deep painful breath. 'I've been such a nuisance to everyone,' she said unhappily. 'I'm sorry. I must at least apologise to him before I go.'

'If you want to see the skipper so much,' Luke went on in an amused tone, 'why don't you come along to the saloon for dinner? There's absolutely no need for you to eat alone in your room all the damned time. I can't understand why you do it. Besides, the other officers would like to see you. Come and dine with us tonight, Faith.'

For the first time Faith really laughed. 'What?' she exclaimed. 'Like this? You may not believe me, Luke, but I have nothing to put on. I've been in this kimono for weeks—hadn't you noticed?'

Luke flicked his eyes frowningly over the slim figure wrapped demurely in an over-large kimono and grinned. 'Oh, I understand now,' he said, and frowned even more deeply. Then his eyes lit up. 'I know what,' he said, and his voice rang with excitement. 'I've got the very thing. I've got a super dress in my trunk, Faith.' He laughed at her expression. 'I bought it for my sister. You can try it on and if it fits you can give us all a treat in the saloon tonight.'

An almost boyish smile covered his face and at last Faith laughed too. 'All right,' she said, and her heart was beating furiously again. 'If the dress fits,' she said tremulously, 'I'll be there. And if you'll let me, I'll buy it from you, Luke. I have a little money.'

'No, it's a present from me, darling.' Luke grinned and gave her a sheepish look. 'I insist.'

'Well, thanks, Luke,' she said, and suddenly she

leant forward and gave him a quick kiss. 'That's for being so nice,' she told him.

'Well, thanks anyhow,' he said, and sighed deeply. 'You'd better come along to my cabin, Faith. I'll fish that dress out now. And there may be one or two more things you would like. There's some perfume.'

'Oh, no!' Faith clapped her hands together joyfully. 'Oh, Luke,' she breathed, 'you are good!'

It took Luke five minutes to get his trunk down and fish out the dress and after leaving her for ten minutes he returned to the cabin to stare at her in amazement. With a whistle, he said, 'You look super, Faith—absolutely super! That dress could have been made for you!' He stood back to assess her appearance carefully, 'Yes,' he said with the air of a connoisseur, 'it's decidedly you. It looks like a dream.'

'It fits me,' Faith returned stiffly and without a smile. 'But there's very little dress.'

'It's sleeveless and has a plunge neckline. What did you want? A hair shirt?'

'Your sister's not frightened of fashion, then?'

'She's with it all the way.'

Faith stared into the long wall mirror. The plunge was too deep, the dress was too skimpy altogether. It was black and cheap-looking, she thought, the material too shiny. But she did not want to hurt or disappoint Luke, so she said, 'I don't think it's me, Luke. Black's not my colour.'

'It's terrific. You look stunning. Black is every girl's colour.' He would not be put off. 'Stack your hair up and put on some make-up. Let's have a party, Faith. We don't want you to turn into a recluse like the old man.'

The old man! A shadow crossed over Faith's still face. 'Luke,' she began again in a sober voice, 'don't you think this dress is just a bit much?'

'Darling, we're not a bunch of choirboys!'

'I know, but——'

'What do you want to look like?' Luke taunted. 'A social worker? Come on, Faith, be a sport.' His smile was appealing. 'Come on, the chaps are all a bit browned off. It would do us all good to see you looking like that.'

'All right!' Faith made up her mind to please him. 'I'll wear it. I'll take the perfume back to my room. I'd better not stay here too long.'

Happily, Luke put the kimono about her shoulders and led her to the door. 'See you at six,' he said. 'And I just can't wait to see their faces!'

He did not have to wait long. When six o'clock came and he saw Faith waiting for him in the accommodation alley, he caught his breath in amazement. 'You look like some exotic model in miniature,' he told her, and could not resist pressing his lips to her cold cheek. 'You're a dish!'

Faith wondered; she knew she had gone mad with the eye make-up and she did not feel easy with all her hair piled into a cloud on top of her head. But she did feel different, and she knew that she did smell beautiful. 'The perfume is out of this world,' she told him, as she gave the air about her a little sniff, 'but I'm still not too sure about this dress.'

'I'm sure,' Luke said with smiling confidence, and steered her on. 'Besides, a girl like you, Faith, should be able to wear anything.'

Two minutes later he was pulling her by the hand into the saloon and announcing gleefully, 'Gentlemen, we have a guest!'

The officers scraped back their chairs and stood up, all visibly startled at the sight of her. Faith smiled weakly and Luke led her to a seat—a seat next to the Captain! She could hear nothing but her own pulse roaring in her ears; she was conscious of no one but Sebastian. She gave him a sidelong glance, but for some reason he went on with his drink, as though he had not seen her.

Surely he was not going to ignore her? Would he humiliate her in front of the men? Faith's hands grew hot, perspiration made the back of her dress, and then the front, cling to her skin. She turned to Sebastian again, helplessly and with angry tears pricking her eyes. He *was* ignoring her.

Frantically Faith sought Luke. He was solicitously pouring her a drink. She fixed her eyes on his slim brown wrist and saw that it was shaking a little and she knew that Luke too was conscious of the Captain's bad manners. The men were silent too—sorry for her, no doubt, she thought. Then Luke brought her drink and sat down next to her, and beneath the heavy table she felt his bony knee giving her an encouraging nudge.

She turned again to the Captain and this time

their eyes met and held. In their depths Faith saw a
cold rebuke. Then, to her astonishment and horror,
Sebastian got to his feet and without a word strode
for the door, leaving behind him only the chilly
silence of cold distaste.

Humiliated and trembling, Faith turned to Luke.
All eyes were upon her now, all smiles upon her
dress. With a feeling of bitterness, she stared down
at herself, then without a word she too got to her
feet. She ran to the door and did not stop running
until she reached her quarters. Then, gasping for
breath, she ran through the office and pushed open
the door into her bedroom.

'In the name of heaven, where did you get it?'

Faith stopped as though before a precipice, and
stared in horror at the man who was standing at the
foot of her bed.

'I got it ... I got it from Luke,' she stammered. 'I
had no other.' Defiantly she held her chin high and
her dove-grey eyes were now a little steely. 'Does it
offend you so much?'

'You have no sense at all. Can I believe that you're
so innocent? So damned unworldly?'

'You don't need to believe anything.'

'Oh, but I do. This still happens to be my ship. I
must look after my men.' He frowned hard at her. 'I
must even look after you—whether you like it or
not. You're in my care.'

'You talk as though I was a child!'

'You are! Nothing but a ridiculous child.' He
paced the floor, eyeing her darkly as he did so. 'I

found that out on the island. I've been cursing my-self ever since.'

'Cursing yourself?' Faith spoke with a kind of pro-vocative defiance now, as though challenging him to contradict his former statement. 'Was I so awful?'

His probing gaze made her heart beat exultantly. 'Don't you understand,' he said under his breath, 'don't you know that the Captain of a ship must hold rein to his feelings? No, you weren't awful at all, just stupidly trusting . . .'

'But I do trust you, Sebastian!'

'As you trusted that other rascal, the one that flew away on his disreputable wings? You're a foolish girl, Faith.' As he stared at her he shook his head slowly, moistening his lips as though he had found his own words uncomfortable. 'You're determined to get into some kind of trouble. You just had to parade yourself cheaply. You just wanted to draw attention to yourself.'

'No, no, I didn't want to do that. I wanted to see *you!*'

His eyes narrowed and for a few moments he stood back to consider Faith, drinking in the loveli-ness of her grave young face, flinching from the sweet earnestness that lay in her eyes. Then he closed the door behind him and walked towards her saying slowly, 'In that case, I must make sure you never want to see me again. I want you out of my life, Faith. You've tormented me ever since that first day out from Singapore. For your own sake, I've got to teach you a lesson.'

Faith stared back at him in amazement. She was not afraid, and yet she had never seen a man look at her with such dark and focused intent. Her heart began to beat fast again, inside her there seemed to be a shower of fireworks. 'Sebastian,' she cried as he gathered her up and carried her to the bed. 'Sebastian! What are you going to do?'

He stared down at her and his wide mouth curved contemptuously. 'Don't tell me a girl wearing such a dress doesn't know!'

'Sebastian!'

It was the inflection in her voice that made him draw his breath quickly and stand back for a moment. Then Faith raised her arms to him and he fell onto the edge of the bed and drew her close to him. 'Sebastian,' she whispered against his cheek, 'I'm not afraid of *you*! I know that *you* could not hurt me.' Looking into his pained eyes she emphasized again, 'I know it.'

'Don't you also know,' he said slowly and deliberately, as he gazed deep into her eyes, 'that all men are liars and all women cheats?'

'I don't believe it.' Faith closed her lips tightly. 'I won't believe it!'

'Haven't you had proof enough?'

For a moment her eyes were shadowed by pain and she lowered her eyelids at the thought of what she had suffered. Then she felt herself being gathered up and Sebastian was kissing her again, just as he had kissed her on the shore at Labuan. She felt no frenzy of fear as he laid her back on the bed and his lips closed over her own; she wanted only to please him, to give herself to him. She lay back, staring up into his eyes, as though stunned by the havoc she knew she had wrought in him. He kissed her again and again, and this time she called out, 'Sebastian! Sebastian! Please ...!'

He broke away and looked down at her, his mouth set in a hard line, the hint of a smile in his narrowed eyes. 'You can take that rag off,' he said in a voice that was barely audible.

'Sebastian?' Dishevelled, her lips trembling, her eyes wide, Faith whispered his name again. 'Sebastian!' It seemed that it was too late for regrets now.

Then to her astonishment he stood up and smiled down at her now in a different way. 'Put your kimono on,' he said, and his voice was infinitely gentle. He gave her a swift, almost paternal kiss, and gently lifted her chin to give her another. 'Don't forget me,' he said, and then, to Faith's amazement, he left the room.

CHAPTER EIGHT

THE *English Rose* had berthed at London Docks and after what seemed like hours, Faith was still waiting in the Captain's office, next to the room which had been her prison for the last few eventful weeks. Surely, she thought anxiously, surely he won't walk away out of my life without even a word of farewell? But it was already two o'clock and the ship was uncannily silent. Most of the men had gone ashore. Even Luke had disappeared and if he did not turn up at any moment there was going to be no time for shopping. And she had to get something to wear! With troubled eyes, she gazed down at her dress, the cheap affair which had brought about such heartache. But she was compelled to wear it, for she had no other.

She began to pace restlessly up and down, shivering a little and clasping her arms as she walked, although the bright September sun gave proof that winter was far away.

At last there was a step outside. It was Luke, smiling his apologies and looking a stranger in his dark blue uniform with its gold ribbon about the sleeves. 'I'm sorry I've been so long, Faith,' he said swiftly. 'One or two things cropped up, but we can go now.' He stared hard at her and raised his eyebrows curiously. 'Are you going to wear that?'

'Of course I am,' Faith flung back at him with a rush of nerves. 'You know very well that I have nothing else. I must get to one of the stores before they're all closed for the night.'

'All right! I've said I'm sorry.' He glanced about the room.

'I haven't any luggage either, if that's what you're looking for,' she exclaimed.

Luke ignored her bitterness, and flicking up his sleeve he glanced at his watch. 'We'll get a taxi into town,' he said happily, 'and then a train to Peterborough.'

'I haven't seen the Captain,' Faith said wearily. 'Has he gone?'

'I expect so. He never wastes any time once we berth.'

'I see.' She gulped and turned to the door. 'Come on, then,' she said in a small voice. She noticed Luke giving her an odd glance and added quickly, 'You look super in full kit, Luke. I'm proud of you.'

'Then cheer up.' Luke put his arm about her shoulders and gave her a squeeze. 'And stop worrying about your dress. It looks fine to me.'

'That was all that was worrying me, Luke,' she returned with mirthless amusement.

'Oh, for heaven's sake!' Luke stood back to frown and sigh. 'If it's the fact that the old man didn't say goodbye that's bothering you, forget it, Faith. I warned you about him. He's not the most mannerly of men.'

For a moment Faith turned back. She knew what Sebastian was like! She could never forget him. She closed her eyes as though hoping when she opened them again to see him there. In her mind's eye she saw his magnificent face, his strong features, his high cheekbones, his black tumbling hair and his steady coffee-brown, assessing eyes. With a sigh she turned back to Luke. Somehow she had to put from her mind for ever the time she had spent on the *English Rose*, the time she had spent on the island, the horror of Sorgre and the joy of Sebastian finding her. It all had to go; there could be no looking back. To think about Sebastian and to know that she would never see him again would be too much of a torment.

Outside it was beginning to rain, and it was raining even harder when they reached the city. The taxi rushed on, splashing quickly through the wet streets. In the back seat, Luke slipped his arm about her. 'Are you cold?' he asked.

'A little.' Faith was still far away.

'Then I must keep you warm.'

Luke's arm tightened about her, but she did not realise it; she sat numb with unhappiness while somewhere in the background Luke raved on about the big city. 'We're going to have a great time,' he told her. 'In fact we needn't rush off to Peterborough straight away. 'I've wired my parents, but we can turn up at any time.'

Still Faith did not hear him. Still she thought about the dark Captain Hilliard. Where was he?

What was he doing? Where was he going? Perhaps he would stay in the city? There was always a chance that they would meet again ...

'Hi there!' Luke said accusingly. 'You're not listening.'

'Sorry, Luke.' Faith forced a smile on to her face. 'And thank you for everything. I really don't know what I would have done without you. All alone in London!' She drew her breath at the horror of it.

'You haven't a headache or anything?'

She shook her head. 'No, I feel fine. Just a little overawed by everything.'

'Good! We'll stop here where all the large stores are.' Luke took out his wallet as he spoke. 'Take this, Faith,' he said assertively. 'Go mad and buy yourself something stunning. I know you don't appreciate my taste.' He grinned and frowned alternatively at her black dress and then laughed, 'I owe it to you,' he said, and pressed a wad of notes into her hand. 'Now don't argue with me,' he protested before she could open her mouth. 'You can pay me back one of these days.'

The taxi stopped and went on and Luke told her, 'I'll give you an hour. Come back to this spot, Faith. I'm just going to have a drink.'

'I'll be here, Luke. And thank you.' Faith's voice was small. 'You really are good.'

But Luke was not listening. Already he had disappeared into the crowds, so she turned to the big city stores with flushed cheeks and eyes full of excitement. Then she started towards one of the large plate-glass doorways.

Most of the young girls she saw wore trousers and gay tops, or even long skirts with matching tops. She bought a pair of lilac needlecord jeans and a matching fine sweater, also a shirt-dress and an inexpensive three-quarter-length cotton raincoat. Then, after buying some make-up, she hurriedly went to the ladies' room where she spent a full half hour transforming herself into a modern city girl.

Luke was delighted with her appearance when she met him, but this time he made no remark. 'We'll go and have something to eat and then we're going out on the town.'

'Luke!' Faith's eyes were full of entreaty now. 'I've got to do something about finding a job and somewhere to stay.'

'There's plenty of time for that,' he told her as he took her arm. 'For goodness' sake, Faith, we're on leave.'

'But Luke——'

'For God's sake!' Luke dragged her back and then grinned. 'Do you want to get me run down on my first day ashore? Take it easy, girl.'

The restaurant he chose was quite a lavish one. 'I'm going to enjoy this,' he said, gazing gleefully across the table at her. 'Now, what would you like to eat, Faith? A good steak? That's what I'm having.'

'Oh, you see to it, Luke. I'm not really hungry.'

'Of course you're hungry. You're having a steak?' He sat back and smiled at the waiter. 'Good,' he said as a bottle of wine was set down on the table. 'I'm just in the mood for a nice sharp drink.'

He had had quite a bit to drink, Faith could see

that by the flush on his face and the brightness of his eyes. But he was plainly enjoying himself and after the meal they made their way to a cinema in Shaftesbury Avenue where they spent an hour or so. Faith sat with her eyes closed most of the time, but she could hear Luke laughing and clapping and it was almost all she could do to stop herself from getting up and running out. But where would she go? She had no real money. Luke meant to be kind to her, but he just did not understand. His hand was fumbling for her own again and this time she snatched it back quite angrily.

'Don't you like it here?' Luke murmured against her cheek.

'Not really.'

'Then we'll go.' He took her hand and pulled her to her feet. 'We'll have another drink, then perhaps you'd like a trip around the city. London's great by night.'

They went to a bar that Luke knew well. The barman hailed Luke heartily. Faith watched the two men have a few words together.

'I've known that chap for years,' Luke told her the moment he returned with the drinks. 'A few fellows I know have been in today. Pity I missed them.' He gave her a warm smile. 'You know,' he said as he sat down, 'I've really enjoyed myself today, Faith.' He drew in his chair and leaned across the table, his eyes appraising.

Something about his smile made her say quickly,

'I hope you'll enjoy all your leave, Luke. You certainly deserve to.'

'Are you really in a hurry to see my parents?' he asked, the strange glint still in his eyes.

'Of course not!' Faith gulped over her words. 'But if we're staying in town, then I'm in a hurry to get fixed up somewhere for the night. There must be a small hotel or somewhere I could book bed and breakfast.'

Luke sat back, a frown on his face now. 'Bed and breakfast,' he said in a tone of disgust, then he laughed. 'I'm sure you don't mean to insult me, Faith,' he went on, leaning forward again, 'but bed and breakfast——! I'm going to book you in at a hotel with me. You're not living in the dark ages, darling. There's no one who's going to disapprove. I'm not exactly repulsive, am I?'

Faith's heart beat warningly now. 'Of course not,' she told him. 'But I'd rather I got booked up somewhere, Luke. I'm tired and I'd prefer it if you had a night on the town on your own. I'd just be a drag. Besides, I really must wash my hair.'

'We'll see,' said Luke, putting his arm round her and signalling to the barman for more drinks. 'Don't worry, Faith, I won't eat you.' He turned back to her smiling mischievously. 'As I said, I'm not repulsive, and everyone can't be in love.'

What could she say? For a moment she closed her eyes. Luke was nice enough. He knew she wasn't in love with him, but he would look after her nevertheless. She swallowed hard and looked up at him again, wondering what to say to him. Suddenly the barman was calling out to him and making wild gestures in the direction of someone further up the narrow room.

'Damn!' Luke said under his breath as he waved to the Second Mate of the *English Rose*. 'I might have known we'd crash into someone from the ship here! Everyone knows this place.'

Relieved at the god-sent interruption, Faith sank back on her chair, wondering what was to happen next, wondering if she should not use this interruption as a chance to escape.

The Second Mate called a greeting and he dragged out a chair and sat down at the table. There was no smile on his face and he gave Faith a brief nod and then ignored her.

'What are you going to drink? What will you have?' Luke was all smiles again, and just a little tipsy. 'Fancy meeting you, Second!'

'I've had all I want, thank you. I'm rushing off to catch a train.'

Faith sat sober-faced; she remembered the Second Mate. He was dark, and rather like Luke, but his eyes were more deeply set. He looked clever, she thought, and careful. She ignored him, as he had done her, and concentrated on her drink.

'I suppose you've heard about the old man?'

The Second's words brought Faith to attention. She swallowed hard and jerked up, listening intently now to what he had to say.

'Heard what?' Luke was asking.

'Something leaked out, apparently,' the Second went on swiftly. 'The old man had trouble getting off the ship. He's had to answer a lot of questions, poor devil. In fact, I think our skipper's in real trouble this time.'

'Trouble?' The words wavered from Faith's lips. 'What kind of trouble?'

The Second Mate sat back to eye Faith curiously. 'It appears that the Bali police are holding an English engineer and a Chinese steward on a drugs charge, and the Chinese is trying to involve the Captain. I'm afraid he told the police about your being on the ship, Miss Charteris. How he'll explain that, I don't know. I only know that he's in a bit of a mess. He could lose his ticket.'

Faith stared back hard at the Second Mate, whose eyes were now accusing, then she stood up shakily. 'We must go back to the ship,' she said to Luke. 'We'll have to do something ...'

'If you've got any sense you'll keep out of that man's way,' the Second Mate said in a voice that made Luke frown. 'Besides,' he went on with a sly wink, 'didn't the old man tell you to get rid of her?' He grinned again as he looked at Faith.

Get rid of her! Faith saw the Second Mate through a blur as he left the bar. Her thoughts whirled in unhappy confusion. Get rid of her— Sebastian had told Luke that! Her lips parted, she raised pained eyes. 'Did he say that?' she asked Luke.

'I always said the Second was a swine,' said Luke,

flopping down again and turning to watch the receding figure of the other man. 'He never could keep his damned mouth shut.'

Faith could barely breathe, but she managed to gasp, 'Did the Captain really tell you to get rid of me, Luke? Did he really?' Her voice shook with emotion. 'Was he still on the ship when we left? You said he'd gone.'

'Yes,' said Luke in a tired voice and reaching for his drink. 'He was still on the ship, Faith. And he was having trouble with the police. You might well have been in trouble had they found you—the Captain knew that.'

Faith got to her feet. 'Luke,' she said urgently, 'you've got to tell me where I can find Captain Hilliard now. I've got to talk to him. If he's in trouble because of me, then I must speak out. If you don't tell me where he's gone, then I must go to the police myself. I don't care what they do to me. They can deport me or send me to prison!'

'You don't know what you're saying,' Luke said hotly, putting down his glass. 'But then,' he went on, leaning over the table and staring directly into Faith's eyes, 'they tell me that people never do when they're in love. Come on, Faith, let's go.'

'I'm not going anywhere until you give me his address,' Faith said determinedly now, through gritted teeth. 'I'm not moving, Luke, until you write it down.'

'Damn you!' Luke sat down heavily and drew out his diary, then his pen. 'Thank God,' he muttered as he began to write, 'that I'm not involved. You go your way now, Faith.'

For almost four hours the train had thundered north, then Faith had managed to get on a bus going on as far as the village called Elsdon. In the pocket of her raincoat was Sebastian's address: Mill House, Elsdon, Northumberland.

There were few passengers on the bus which drove north on its way almost to the Border hills, and within an hour Faith had been put down outside a village pub called the Bird in the Bush at the village of Elsdon, a quaint place with ancient tower and church and houses gathered about the village green, with the undulating fells leading away from all sides up to a wide, wild skyline.

The yawning country driver directed her to the Hilliards' house and after waving goodbye to him she started on her way across the green, and then down the bank to the bridge and the house.

It was a silent, silvery village and far away from the port of Singapore, the island of Labuan and the village which for some odd reason had been called Heaven. The air was soft and clean, everything around seemed unreal to Faith; she felt as though she walked in a dream, but a happy dream. In this village she knew that there were no evil spirits. It was a beautiful night, and the quaint English village slept below its overlay of moonshine while the distant hills kept guard.

Walking on, she disturbed a band of sleeping

geese and they rose protesting loudly before they sank down again. An owl hooted eerily from its perch on a tree close by the churchyard and another fell bird cried lonesomely, but Faith was not afraid. She was calm and soothed by the serenity of the night and by the fact that she would soon be with Sebastian. She refused to allow him to get into any serious bother because of herself; that was what she had travelled all those miles to tell him.

For a few minutes she paused to think of her mother and the childhood she must have enjoyed in such a village, and the tears came momentarily to her eyes. She glanced back at the moonlit green and, reassured, walked on.

Soon she was staring up at the house called Mill House, which stood close by to the river. The air was full of the fragrance of scented stock, honeysuckle and lavender, and smiling as she breathed in the different perfumes, she slowed her steps to gaze over the gates into the well-kept garden. It was a stately-looking Victorian house, standing in its own grounds, but what made Faith stare so much was the fact that it was so brilliantly lit up. Most of the windows blazed with light and yet there was no sound, no sign of life.

Her face set with anxiety again. Perhaps she should not have acted so impulsively? Should she turn back now and try to get a room for the night at The Bird in the Bush? Perhaps they were having a party at Mill House, she thought with a fresh rush of horror—and she was about to gatecrash! She stood back to stare at the name on the painted white gate again. Yes, it was Mill House all right; she had come to the right place.

For a few minutes she stood shivering beneath the moon, then she made up her mind and pushed open the gate. She had come a long way to find Sebastian, and find him she would. For a moment she paused again, but this time only to listen to the dreamy sound of the water on its lazy way and to stare at the great squares of light projected eerily onto the wide lawns. Then, like someone in a dream, Faith glided up to the door.

Surprisingly, it stood wide open. She wondered what she should do. At last, with a shaking hand, she determinedly lifted the black wrought-iron knocker, let it drop, and stood back quickly to listen to its hollow thud resounding through the house. When the sound had completely died away, she knocked again.

But no one came in answer to the summons. After a few anxious minutes, Faith stepped warily over the threshold and peered into the wide hall.

'Captain Hilliard!' she called nervously at first. And then more bravely, 'Captain Hilliard! Are you at home?'

The house remained silent. Faith felt scared now and she stood clasping her arms about her. Then something took her attention and again she peered into the brightly lit hall. Two large suitcases which she recognised stood against one of the walls. She had come to the right house. This was Sebastian's home. A wave of thankfulness swept over her and again she went back to bring the iron knocker down with all her might this time.

Still there was no movement, no sound, and she moved into the hall and then up to the door nearest to her. It stood ajar and she pushed it a little and peered in.

It looked like a study; the walls were lined with bookshelves and a redwood desk stood in front of the window. The walls were painted white and an enormous oil painting of the hills, huntsmen and heather-clad fells drew Faith's attention. Then she heard a sound of a movement somewhere in the house and she quickly retraced her steps into the hall. She strained her ears again, but once again the house was silent.

'Captain Hilliard! Captain Hilliard!'

Faith called again and again, but there was no reply other than that of the echo of her own tremulous voice. But she had heard something! There was someone in the house. Her heart was drumming fearfully again. She glanced up, strained her ears and listened intently. Then it came again—a soft tapping noise on the ceiling above her. She gasped with alarm. Someone in the room above was trying to draw her attention. They could be sick. Something was very wrong! It could be Sebastian.

She found the stairs and hurried up them, then ran quickly along the wide landing to where one of the doors stood partly open. With thudding heart she peered into the bedroom and then stared in dismay at the figure she saw lying on the bed, and gasping for her breath. Then she pulled herself together and hurried to the bedside.

She thought the young woman who lay on the bed, propped up by pillows, was about the loveliest creature she had ever seen. She had more than mere prettiness, for there was character and intelligence in the strongly moulded face. Her mouth was sensitive and her enormous lavender blue eyes and the pool of corn-gold hair that lay on the pillow behind her made Faith catch her breath in admiration. She realised that the woman had been suffering from an acute asthma attack, for her eyes were stricken and her face drawn, and in her hands she tightly gripped some kind of instrument which she had been obviously using to ward off the attack. But she seemed quieter now, and as Faith stared at her another thought came into her mind, one that sent her reeling. She gripped the bed-end and tried to calm her own breathing. The woman in the bed was beautiful—and also about Sebastian's age. She was in his house ... and his bed! Was this the reason, she wondered, why Luke had always maintained that the Captain had no interest in women? Had he, all the time, been married to this lovely woman?

'It's all right, it's passing off.' The woman in the bed smiled weakly and then asked, 'Were you passing by? I'm sorry if I gave you a fright.'

Faith gulped and shook her head. 'I'm looking for Captain Hilliard,' she said in a small voice. 'I came here to find him. I got no answer, and then I heard you tapping and so I came in.'

'I see. How did you know Sebastian would be

here?' The woman considered Faith with surprise in her eyes. 'He's just arrived home tonight after a long trip.'

'Is there anything I can do for you?' Faith asked on a long breath. 'Can I get you a drink?'

'No, no.' The woman smiled pleasantly again. 'I'll be perfectly all right in about half an hour.' She laughed a little and then went on, 'I must pretty myself up. Of all nights to have an asthma attack!' She struggled up and peered about the room and then back at Faith again. 'Do you live in the village?' she asked, but absently.

Numbly, Faith shook her head.

'I see,' the woman went on in a puzzled voice and one which meant she did not. 'Then if you have something to say to Sebastian, I suggest you walk over to The Bird in the Bush. He's there having a drink—or he may have left. In that case you'll meet him on the green.'

'I think I should ring for your doctor,' Faith suggested swiftly. 'I'd feel better if I did so.'

'Nonsense!' The woman frowned at her this time. 'I'm used to these attacks. It's the high pollen count, you know. But the worst is over, I feel much better. There's no need for you to worry.' She paused to consider Faith again, then she asked, 'Would you like me to give Sebastian a message?' She laughed before Faith could answer and said, 'I expect you've come to ask him to open a fête. He always opens one or two when he's on leave.'

'No,' Faith said quickly, nervously straining her

ears for any sound of returning footsteps downstairs. 'I'll telephone him.'

'Well, it is a bit late, and he has just arrived home.'

The expression in the woman's blue eyes made Faith turn away. 'If you insist that you're all right,' she said swiftly, and as she reached the door, 'then I'll go.' And as fast as her legs could carry her, she left the room and went downstairs with a terrible feeling of nausea. She had to get away, quickly. She would get a taxi from somewhere and go anywhere. Anywhere would do so long as she never again had to face Sebastian Hilliard. Knowing that he had such a wife it was going to be sheer torture even to think about him, to remember what he had been to her. She felt in her pocket for the money Luke had given her and blessed him for it. With money she would be able to get a taxi anywhere—at any time.

'I'm sure he won't be long ... Perhaps you should wait?'

The voice faded as Faith hurriedly made her way outside ... faded as the last vestige of hope now faded in her heart. Her breath came fast, her eyes were tragic as she started down the steep staircase. She stepped into the hall and then stopped dead, the blood draining away from her, as she came face to face with Sebastian.

CHAPTER NINE

'FAITH!' He clasped her wrists with strong fingers. 'Faith!'

Tight-lipped and sober-eyed, Faith struggled free of his grasp and stared back at him, trying desperately to see him as the cheat he was and not the devastatingly dynamic man who stood before her in neat dark uniform and immaculately laundered shirt. But try as hard as she did, she could not bring the shutters down against him completely; even now she felt the excited beat of her heart, the strain of desire.

He stepped forward again and this time his hands closed over her slim shoulders. 'Faith, what is it?' This time his eyes were curious, his dark brow furrowed as he studied her face.

Faith closed her eyes; she could not look at him, her weakness was too great, the confusion in her mind too deceiving. She wanted to fall into his arms, but knew she could not. She thought of the beautiful woman waiting up in her bedroom for him and the thought gave her the strength to struggle free again.

'I've just come from The Bird in the Bush,' he said in a puzzled tone. 'I got a telephone call from Webb. He told me that you'd followed me north,

Faith.' This time he brought down his heavy eye-lids as he smiled slowly. 'I couldn't believe it.'

'I can't believe it either,' Faith said in a dull monotone and still avoiding his eyes. 'I've wasted my time, Captain Hilliard. I find I have nothing to say to you after all. I made a mistake ...' Her voice began to waver and she could not go on.

'Another?' His deep voice was gentle and tinged with humour. 'My dear child,' he went on softly. 'It's quite apparent that you need someone to look after you. You obviously can't look after yourself.'

'I must go. I must find somewhere to stay for the night.' Faith's voice shook as she turned to go.

Sebastian caught her arm and this time detained her roughly, telling her in a tone she could well re-member, 'Don't be ridiculous, child. How can you possibly find anywhere at this time? Besides, you came all this way to see me. You apparently have something to tell me. So calm down and be sensible,' his lips stirred into a smile, 'even if it is for the first time in your life.' Firmly he drew her back, his arm about her shoulders. 'I can understand you being furious over the fact that I had to ask Webb to get you off the ship. But there were mitigating circum-stances which I did ask him to explain. You surely understand that, Faith?'

She slid away from his arm. 'I understand every-thing now,' she told him, and this time she raised defiant eyes to his. 'I understand men. I know that they're all deceitful as well as selfish. Even Luke,' she went on sadly. 'He told me nothing at all.' And with a sigh she went on, 'But I can look after myself and I'm certainly not going to stay in this house, so don't ask me, Captain Hilliard—I refuse to do so. I'm going now. I'll get a taxi somewhere.'

'Faith!' This time his voice was a sharp command. 'Stay where you are,' he went on in a daunting tone, 'and for God's sake tell me what's happened. If I seem to have offended you, then I'm sorry. Do you expect me to get down on my knees and ask you to forgive me? I told the First Mate to tell you that I'd get in touch. I made it quite plain.' He sighed impatiently. 'It isn't always easy to captain a ship,' he told her more gently, 'but I did my best to look after you, Faith. I even managed to keep hold of the rein to my own feelings.' He shrugged his shoulders. 'Well, shall we say for most of the time?'

'Maybe,' Faith said in a voice she hoped sounded just as daunting, 'but there happens to be someone upstairs waiting for you, Captain.'

'Oh, yes, Gloria!' He flicked a glance towards the stairs.

'For your information, Gloria has had a bad asthma attack while you've been away drinking and telling the locals what a great trip you've had.'

Something in his face changed as he stared hard at Faith and then, with a curse, he strode away towards the stairs. 'I might have known this would happen,' he roared back. 'And you're right for once, Miss Charteris—I should never have left her.' His voice grew harsh, almost cruel as he flung back, 'But there's one thing certain, I never will again!'

Faith lost no time after that in running out of the house and down the garden path to the road. Never in her life had she ever felt so hurt, so stripped of dignity. But never before had she ever loved anyone so much! If he had been the devil, she thought despairingly, she would still have loved him.

As she ran, she grew frightened. Everything seemed to have taken on a nightmarish quality. Even the trees and shrubs etched stark in the moonlight menaced her. The silence was overpowering. Cobwebs turned about her throat in a frail effort at strangulation, and then something brushed against her and whirred away again and she knew that it had been a bat. She cried out this time and began to run as fast as she could towards the village green.

Once in the pub, she began to feel better. It was a pleasant place and filled with chattering folk who had come from the town to spend a cheerful evening in a village pub. Someone accosted her, but she ignored him and pushed her way to the bar counter where a brisk, kindly-faced woman was serving drinks.

'I want a taxi,' Faith said at once, breathlessly. 'Do you know where I could get one? I want to get to Newcastle.'

'Yes, love. Charlie Graham will give you a lift at any time and at any hour. He's round the corner. You can't miss him—the first house.'

'Oh, thank you! Thank you!' Greatly relieved, Faith gave the woman a smile, then pushed her way to the door again. Round the corner, the first house. She could not miss him. Outside, the smell of cut grass all about her, she began to run again.

She came to the corner and started up a narrow moonlit track, her eyes wide and alert as she looked round for a house. She walked for five minutes and still there was no house. Once again everything began to look eerie. Small patches of mist rose like ghosts and the air seemed to have a humid warmth. It clung clammily to her skin and as she walked she had to keep dodging clouds of night insects.

No house appeared. It finally dawned on Faith that she must have turned the wrong corner after leaving The Bird in the Bush. She should have turned right and instead she had taken the left turn. She slowed down as she walked over a hump-backed bridge, then hurried on as another cloud of midges arose. Up the road she could see a small house and she began to run again, deciding to ask the people at the house for fresh direction.

But the house, which had seemed so close, was really far away and, after hurrying along the fell road for more than ten minutes, Faith found that she was no closer. Panting, she stopped and glanced back down into the valley, and straightened up instantly, recoiling in dismay. The village seemed to have completely disappeared and a dense sea of fog now almost filled the valley. Not a house was to be seen, not a tree. There were only the black distant hills beyond and ahead of her the rising fells and the lonely house. Faith's own vision blurred with fear for a moment, then turning, she began to run uphill again. She had to get to the house. Her heart was beating fast, her blood rushing through her veins in a spate of terror. She stumbled, picked herself up again ... and then there was the house, tumble-down—and quite deserted.

Faith sat down on the edge of a crumbling wall to get her breath. There was nothing she could do, she told herself, but watch the fog creep up the hill. Eventually she would be enveloped like everything else. She could keep on running, but the mists would follow her; they would follow her up all the way to the vast night sky. There seemed to be nothing but the thick rolling fog beneath her and the black vast sky above her. And she was alone, without even a friend and in a strange land.

'But I can't just sit here!' she cried suddenly, giving way to a burst of hysteria. 'I must go on. There must be a farmhouse somewhere!'

She began to sob a little as she walked, but she quickly rubbed the tears of self-pity away with the back of her hand, and strained her eyes in the silvery light for the sign of a farmhouse.

The narrow country road wound its way up the fellside for mile after mile and eventually Faith flung herself down on a verge of rough grass. She was exhausted, she could go no further. For a while she closed her eyes and contemplated her future. That was if there was going to be a future for her, she reminded herself despairingly. She knew all about the changing moods of the weather in the north of

England. She remembered how her mother had told her that if a wind got up a person lost on the moors could die of exposure. But her thoughts hurried on. If she did survive, she would return to London and get a job as a typist. Then she would save until she had enough money to get a passage back to Singapore. She nursed no dream now, she could face stark reality. For her, there was to be no white Christmas, no quiet life in an English village. She was hardened now and she trusted no one, not even Luke. But she found herself sighing all the same, for she knew, hard as she might try to hate Sebastian Hilliard, she would still go on loving him.

She got up and drew in a painful breath of moorland air. She had to keep on going, she told herself; she couldn't sit there dreaming. She walked on and then the going became rough and she realised that the road had petered out and that she was now walking on sharp stones. Heather brushed harshly against her legs. What was even worse was the fact that low clouds had suddenly drawn away the moon and now it was very dark. She walked a few more hesitant steps, then stopped again. She could not see a thing; everything had been snuffed out. It was pitch black —and she had no idea where she was.

She was so tired. Almost uncaringly, she began to move again. She stumbled once, and twice. Her steps became more hesitant. Somewhere in the distance she heard a dog bark—or was it a fox? she wondered. As she wondered she took another step ... an unlucky one. The stones rattled away from her feet and she felt herself falling and falling. As she fell she screamed, 'Sebastian! Sebastian!'

But there was no one to hear Faith's desperate call. Only the fox on the rim of the fell, calling to his mate on the other side of the copse, and he bounded on, uncaring.

It was over a week later when Faith opened her eyes and peered at the sunlight that filtered through the windows of her room. But as yet no sunlight filtered into the dark, closed recesses of her mind. She knew that she had been in hospital, that the doctor and nurses had been kind and that a specialist had told her not to worry, that everything would suddenly click back and she would remember everything again. The fair-haired specialist had told her that she had been lucky and that she could easily have fractured her skull after such a fall.

What fall? Faith sighed and strained to remember. And where had she fallen? Had she been in an accident? Had she been climbing somewhere? She could not remember. With an acute sense of misery and frustration she stared about the unfamiliar room. Her head still ached fearfully and the sunlight in the room was almost too strong. But it was warm and in some way comforting, so she settled her head back on her pillow and closed her eyes again.

Five minutes later she opened her eyes again. She could not sleep; she could not think, because she had nothing to think about. She stared about the room and thought how gracious it was. It was spacious and the ceiling was high, with an ornamented centrepiece. The windows were high and long and the sunlight caught the long leaves of an enormous potted plant which was on a stand near them. She turned her head a little and saw that a solid oak chest stood against one of the walls and that a Hepplewhite-style chair with a seat of green velvet stood by the bed. In front of the marble fireplace there was a sofa covered with the same velvet that was on the chair and the grate of the fireplace was filled with some enormous ferns. There was a long-pile carpet on the floor and the wallpaper was a pretty country style, which seemed to blend with the earthy fragrance which drifted through the open windows.

Where was she? Her mind strained desperately again. She was not at home, she knew that. They had told her that she was going to friends. But who were these friends who had been kind enough to bring her to their lavish home? She felt herself panicking again and closed her eyes tightly, as though to escape from something dreadful, yet knowing she could not. How her head ached!

The door opened and without opening her eyes Faith knew that someone was softly approaching her bed. She knew it would be the lady with the golden-blonde hair and the large lavender blue eyes who had been looking after her. She tried to speak to her.

'Good morning, Faith!' The woman's voice was gentle, encouraging. 'How do you feel this morning?

Do you feel like getting up or would you like to sleep a little longer?' With a smile she added, 'Sebastian is busy making us an early cup of tea.'

Sebastian? Who was Sebastian? And why was *he* so kind? Faith could not speak, but she nodded and stared hard at the woman who stood at her bedside. She thought she looked very beautiful and she admired her white-quilted housecoat. She was a sophisticated woman, Faith thought, as she continued to study her. Her hair was beautifully groomed, she was expertly made up and her long slim hands were well cared for. There was something nice about her voice too; it was deep yet soft and somehow familiar. 'I'll get up as soon as I've had a cup of tea,' she said with an effort, still straining her mind in an endeavour to remember. 'I just hope I'm not giving you too much trouble. But I'm sure I'll soon be all right again.'

'You mustn't worry, Faith. You must try to relax and leave everything to Sebastian and myself. We have our instructions, we know what to do. All you have to do is remember that you're with friends. We'll do all we can for you.'

Friends! Faith drew her breath and turned away. Why was she with friends? Where were her own people? And if she was so ill, why hadn't they kept her in hospital? She held her head for a moment as though her thoughts were too much for her.

The woman in the white housecoat said quickly, 'Don't try to think, Faith. Just drift. It will all come back—the specialist said it would.'

Faith asked, 'What time is it? I must get up. I must get out of this bed.' She shook her head in an effort to feel more awake.

'It's eight o'clock,' the woman said, then with a laugh she added, 'And as you've obviously forgotten, my name is Gloria.'

'I hadn't forgotten,' Faith lied. 'I'm going to get up now. I won't wait for the tea. Tell ... What was his name?'

'Sebastian?'

'Yes. Tell Sebastian not to bother.'

'Too late,' Gloria laughed as she turned to the door. 'Here he is now, so we must really drink his tea.' She exchanged a glance with the man who had come into the room and indicated with her hand that he must set the tray down on the bedside table.

Faith sat up a little to watch the stranger who called himself a friend, and at once she felt tongue-tied and awestruck. There was something strangely intimidating about this tall, dark man who wore casual trousers and an open-necked shirt. For some reason Faith's heart began to beat very fast and her breath came in nervous little spurts. It was as though her body recognised the man, even if her brain rejected him.

'Tea up,' Sebastian Hilliard said as his eyes went straight to the wisp of a girl in the large bed—a girl with a thin, pale face, dove-grey eyes, one of which was badly bruised. And in a teasing, humorous tone, 'Just when are you going to admit that we've met?'

'I'm sorry,' Faith whispered, turning her eyes

from him. 'I can't remember who you are. I don't know.'

'But you will ... so sit up and be a good girl and drink this tea.'

Faith did sit up, but now her eyes were angry. 'You're talking to me as though I was an idiot,' she flung accusingly. 'I may have forgotten a few things, but you needn't humour me. I'm not a child.'

'Perhaps not ... but you have a habit of acting like one, I'm afraid.'

His voice was infinitely tender and Faith fought the new fear that was rising up in her. Perhaps she was an idiot? Perhaps the hospital had been unable to do anything for her? Perhaps she was never going to get better. Alarm filled her eyes as she stared first at Sebastian and then at the woman who stood at his side. 'I will get better?' she whispered agonisingly. 'You're sure?'

'As sure as the specialist, Faith. So just try to keep calm and trust us.'

'Yes, I will ...' Faith went on hesitantly, 'If you're so sure. I am grateful to you both.'

She met the dark eyes which somehow seemed to burn right down into the recesses of her mind. Where had she met this man? And why did he have such an effect upon her physically? He was uncommonly handsome; dynamic in his dark way. But she could not look into his eyes; she kept on evading them. Something about the stranger both fascinated and repelled her.

She took the cup and saucer he gave her with

shaking hands and stared down hard into the tea which it contained. Then the woman spoke and, glancing up, Faith saw that the man called Sebastian had put his arm about her in a comforting gesture. They were nice people, she thought, very happily married, very well suited to each other. Beautiful people! Yet for some reason she felt acutely embarrassed and wished they would go and leave her to drink her tea alone.

'If you want anything,' the blonde woman said gently, as though she read Faith's unhappy mind, 'just call. We're not far away.'

Faith nodded and gave the man called Sebastian a quick glance. She was acutely conscious of the pull inside her towards him. 'Thank you,' she whispered again. She glanced at the window. 'I'll have a walk later on. Perhaps the fresh air and the sunlight will do something for me.'

'I'm sure it will, dear.'

Faith watched them move to the door, then she called, 'You didn't tell me. Where did I fall? What was I doing?'

She watched them exchange glances again, then the woman said in an aside, 'I'll get your breakfast, Sebastian. You stay and have a little talk with Faith.'

'Tell me,' Faith demanded as she watched the dark, handsome stranger return to her bedside, 'I must know.' Her head still ached and she felt unusually irritable again, almost angry for no reason at all. 'Well, don't just stand there staring at me,' she said suddenly. 'Tell me. I want to know.'

'You were walking on the moors,' he said deliberately, his eyes never leaving her. 'The mist came down and you went over the side of an old disused quarry. You were lucky you didn't fracture your skull. You're lucky to be alive, Faith.'

'Who found me?' she asked in a small, barely audible voice. 'Someone must have found me.'

'Someone out walking found you. But we'll talk about that at some other time. The main thing is to keep calm, sleep and relax as much as you can. You'll remember everything yourself in good time, Faith.'

She nodded and then asked, 'How long have I been here?'

'Just a day or two. You were in hospital for a week. At one time they thought you might need surgery, but you were lucky. It was just bad concussion. Now you must give your head a rest, Faith. Trust me.'

'How can I trust you?' She opened her eyes wide and frowned at him. 'I don't know you.'

'But I know you, Faith.'

Again she felt her whole being lean towards the man at her side, but her head was aching too much to worry and she closed her eyes and sighed. She heard him pick up the tray and then quietly leave the room.

Faith did not get up for her breakfast or anything else. She fell asleep again and when she awoke the room was dim and a fire burned softly in the grate. She raised herself a little and saw that the handsome, dark man was lying back easily on the sofa, smoking a cigar and watching her through the smoke that rose from it. He wore a light jacket and an open-necked checked shirt and she thought how strong and intelligent he looked. There was something cool and very disciplined about him. For a few minutes Faith lay very still, silently considering him from beneath lidded eyes, then she struggled up a little and in a moment he was at her side.

She stared up at him, watching his dark, peat-coloured eyes, and at once her heart was hammering again, her whole being flooded with some strange elation. Her face creased up in her desperate endeavour to identify him. But she could not; she could not remember, so she turned away from him again in despair.

'So much for your walk,' he said in a deep, humorous tone that made her wince with fury again. 'But never mind, I'm sure the long sleep will have done you much more good, Faith.'

'I don't feel any different.' She would not look at him. Again she felt like exploding with anger for no reason at all. 'If you'll excuse me, I must get up. In any case,' she glanced up at him, 'is there any reason why you should sit there? I'm not dying, you know.'

Ignoring her outburst, he said calmly, 'Now you're awake I think you should try to eat something. Gloria has prepared something light for you.'

Gloria! That was the good-looking woman! 'That's kind of her,' she said quickly, and for some reason her hands moved up to her hair and she frowned again. Someone had brushed back her hair and then plaited it. She felt the heavy ugliness of the plait that fell down against her neck. 'I must do something about my hair,' she said nervously.

'Of course!' He was smiling gently. 'That's certainly a good sign. When a woman begins to think about her hair, then she must be getting better.'

Faith frowned down at the lilac nightgown with its exquisite lace edging; she could not remember it either. It certainly did not belong to her; it was so large, it was falling off at her shoulders. She dragged it round her and sat with her hands crossed on her chest.

'Well, I can see you're not going to need my assistance this time.' He moved away.

'This time?' Faith shot the words at him. 'I sincerely hope you've never had to carry me about.' Her words were sharp and she set her mouth primly, as though to imply that she did not appreciate that kind of humour.

He turned back and raised one bushy eyebrow. 'I'll tell Gloria you're awake,' he said slowly and with an even slower smile. 'She'll be delighted.'

'What time is it?' she asked.

'Midnight.'

'Why isn't she in bed?'

'We thought you would awaken.'

'You're very kind.' Ashamed now, Faith slid down the bed a little. 'I don't mean to sound ungrateful ... I just feel so awful, so bad-tempered.' She thrust her head up again. 'Have you been sitting there very long?' she asked curiously. She frowned again, 'I'm not *that* ill, am I?'

'No, of course not. But the specialist did say that everything would snap back and I'd like someone to be with you when it does, Faith. I don't want you to get a fright.'

'Why would I get a fright? Have I done something awful?'

He laughed again as he turned to the door. 'Not awful,' he said gently. 'Just ridiculous. You're a ridiculous girl, Faith.'

'Am I?' She let her head go back again. 'Please tell Gloria to go to bed,' she said in a tired voice. 'I really couldn't eat a thing. I just want to sleep again. I'll get washed and brush my hair later, Please, go to bed.'

'All right, Faith.'

His voice held a deep tenderness that made the tears rush to her eyes and she hastily buried her face into the pillow. Just for a moment she felt sure that he had smoothed her head with the back of his hand, and for some reason she did not dare look up. He was a wonderful man! And his wife was wonderful too! If only she could remember; if only she knew who they were. She wondered why he had come back to stroke her hair.

But Faith was tired and she did not really care. She closed her eyes and within minutes was sleeping again. But this time it was an uneasy sleep and she struggled and tossed, and when she awoke again she saw that there was no one in the room and that it was flooded with moonlight and as light as day. She raised herself up a little and sat gazing from one sharply etched object to another, then slowly she turned to the table at the bedside—and this time her eyes stayed riveted and her heart was suddenly booming in her chest. She felt her breath being whisked away from her as she continued to stare. For in a small glass vase on the table stood a single bloom. In the moonlight it looked ethereal in its beauty. And it was a rose. But Faith did not see it as one; she saw an orchid—a single orchid with crumpled dove-grey petals!

In a flash everything came back to her; her brain was well again. It was like an explosion of fireworks in her head and involuntarily she called out, 'Sebastian! Sebastian!' She remembered everything, everything up to her walk on the moors and the terrifying mist. But foremost in her mind she remembered her love for Sebastian. She called again, frantically, 'Sebastian! Sebastian!'

And Sebastian came. He stood in the open doorway with the moonlight full on his handsome face, and Faith saw that his eyes were fierce with gladness. She raised her hands to him and he came forward, and as he reached her side she looked up and saw revealed in his dark eyes the intensity which she adored. 'Sebastian!' she whispered, and her lips parted softly, in sheer ecstasy. Flooded with the shame and joy of her feelings, she raised her arms to him and he gathered her up as he sat down on the edge of the bed, and she whispered tremulously, tearfully against his hard cheek, 'I love you! I love you! I can't help loving you!' She kept on staring at him, studying his face ... then she remembered, too, that he had a wife, a beautiful, intelligent wife, and she drew back.

'Of course you do! And I love you! For what other reason would a man suffer all this damned inconvenience? For what other reason would you play such a dangerous game?' His voice was warm and husky with emotion. He kissed her tenderly again, smoothing back her hair and drawing his lips across her brow. Then, taking her face between his hands, he pressed his mouth to her parted lips and drew her as close as he dared without hurting her.

Full of joy, Faith gazed back into his eyes and with a rush of passion she whispered, 'Oh, Sebastian, I must tell you now. I came here to tell you that whatever happens, you mustn't lose your Captain's ticket because of me. I'm determined to face the authorities with you.' Her voice rose and shook with concern, as she drew him down to her again. 'Luke and I met your Second Mate in London and he told us all about it.'

'And you got on a train and came all the way to Mill House to find me?'

She nodded, and his lips met her tremulous ones. 'Of course,' she whispered. 'What else was I to do? I won't allow them to ruin your career because of me.'

'And I won't have you involved because of that

devil Jeremy Caithness, Faith. You don't understand how serious this charge is going to be. It's criminal! Believe me, that scoundrel will involve you if he can. No, you must leave this to me.'

'Why didn't you tell me?' Faith raised her face to be kissed again. 'Why did you just let me go away?'

'I told Luke to tell you I'd contact you as soon as I could.'

'He didn't tell me that.'

'Of course he didn't!' He laughed low in his throat and laid a hard cheek against hers. 'I was a fool to imagine he would.'

Perhaps Luke had meant it for the best, Faith thought with a pang of guilt, and drew back from his arms. The man she adored, loved with all her heart and being, already had a wife.

She closed her eyes and without knowing it sighed as though her heart would break. Sebastian, seeing the shadow which had fallen across her pale face, said quickly and with anxiety, 'This is unforgivable of me! I must be losing my senses.' But his lips stirred into a smile again as he stooped down to cover Faith gently with the bedclothes. 'If I don't let you settle down and get to sleep again I'm going to be the man responsible for your next relapse!'

Faith stirred a little and gazed up again into the magnificent eyes of the man she loved. Then, goaded by the fact that he must leave her, she suddenly thrust up her arms in a desperate effort to keep him. She clung to him desperately and because she knew that he could never tell her that he loved her, she whispered passionately, 'Kiss me again! Oh, Sebastian, kiss me.' Sinking back, she drew him to her, treasuring the strange smile in his dark, impenetrable eyes, the gentleness of his strong hands. She loved him. She wanted to shout out her love, but she knew she could not.

Sebastian kissed her tenderly, then firmly he covered her and stood up again, then noticing again the sadness in her eyes, he said hesitantly, 'Faith, is there anything wrong? Anything you haven't told me about?'

She stared back at him in wistful concentration for a few moments, then she turned her eyes away from him. Everything was wrong, but she could never tell him. 'You'd better go,' she murmured. 'Tell Gloria that I'm well again and that I can remember everything.'

He gave her one last swift kiss, his gaze lingering upon her young throat and shoulders with a candour that set her heart pounding again. 'Be a good girl,' he told her in a low caressing tone. 'Remember, Faith, we have all the future,' his smile was teasing, his heavy eyelids lowered, 'so don't let's run any risks. You might even have another brainstorm —stow away on a ship—or do some other ridiculous thing like chasing some attractive villain half way across the world.'

Faith tugged at his hand. 'Or swim naked in a sun-drenched lagoon,' she capped with a frivolity she by no means felt.

'Yes, you might even do that,' he said slowly as he drew away from her. 'Fortunately, I'll be here to see that you're never left alone again, Faith, to make such silly mistakes.'

And, so saying, he left her to rest.

Faith eventually fell asleep again, and when she awakened it was bright day and everything had fallen back into true perspective. There was now no dreamy moonlight to delude her; facts stabbed in her head like tiny spearheads.

She got up and quickly drawing a light dressing gown about her shoulders made her way to the bathroom. She was going to look her best when she said goodbye to Sebastian. She had to say goodbye, she knew that. His kisses and caresses could not eclipse the fact that he was a married man. She had no intention of staying on at his house.

In the enormous bathroom at the end of the landing, Faith recoiled in horror as she stared into a large wall mirror. She stared back at herself in dismay. Once again one of her eyes was badly bruised. Her hair hung in one awful, ugly plait. So this was how she had looked when Sebastian had kissed her! For a while Faith continued to stare at her reflection in horror, then she quickly flung off her dressing gown and turned on the bath tap, determined to do something about herself. And half an hour later when Gloria came into the bedroom she had to pause and gasp with surprise at the girl who now sat on the edge of the bed looking frail and nervous but extremely lovely with her hair brushed out and hanging sleek and lustrous round her shoulders, her fragile face made up just enough to hide the fact that her features had had a rather rough time.

Gloria set down the breakfast tray and said at once, 'Faith, I can hardly believe it. You look lovely —so sweet! As for that black eye, the bruising has almost subsided. And of course, Sebastian has told me the good news. You're well again just as the doctor said you would be.'

'I'm prone to black eyes, Gloria,' Faith said in a small voice but with little mirth. 'I'm just sorry I've had to put you to so much trouble. You've been very kind. And I am grateful.'

'My dear, you've been no trouble at all. Now that you're better, we're delighted. We'll be able to enjoy your company.' Gloria glanced at the tray. 'In fact, I should imagine you'd rather come down and have breakfast with Sebastian and myself. You look so much better. Of course, you'll have to be careful for some time, you know.'

'I'm perfectly all right now,' Faith returned, fighting to sound cheerful. 'I'll make my plans as quickly as possible, Gloria. I'll get in touch with Luke. He's the First Mate on the *English Rose*, and I did promise to meet his parents.'

'His parents?' Gloria Hilliard's throat worked a little as she stood still to study Faith more intently. 'You're good friends, then?'

'Oh, yes,' Faith laughed. 'Luke and I have been friends for some time. I suppose Sebastian has told you the story of how I stowed away on his ship.'

Gloria smiled, but only briefly. 'Yes, he did,' she

said rather flatly. 'He's told me lots of things about you, Faith. In fact, I'd rather hoped that you'd be staying with us for a while. Have you got to rush off?'

'I'd like to speak to Luke,' Faith said quickly, and then turning to the breakfast tray, she added, 'I'll just eat my breakfast here, Gloria. And thank you for bringing it up. I'll have to make all this up to you in some way.' She glanced after Gloria, who had walked stiffly to the door. 'Sebastian knows Luke's telephone number. Would you ask him to get him for me?'

'Of course!'

The door closed and Faith frowned at the attractive breakfast tray, at the single flower in the tiny vase, and bit her lip to stem her tears. Gloria would think that she could not wait to get away. But it was not like that at all. To stay would be fatal. She both respected and admired Gloria Hilliard; she refused to deceive her in even the smallest way. Slowly Faith crossed to the dressing table, where she stood staring back into her own leaden eyes. If she stayed at Mill House a day longer she knew she would weaken. She knew how much she loved Sebastian and so she had to go now, while she had the strength of character to do so. Even though she knew that she must grieve for ever for her lost love.

Faith could not eat, but she drank some coffee very slowly, then turned in alarm when the door opened and Sebastian came heavily into the room. She stood up and they faced each other in silence. Sebastian was the first one to raise a smile and he strode over and sat down on the edge of the bed, reaching up as he did so to catch Faith's hand. 'Don't worry,' he said in a reassuring voice. 'Don't look so distressed, Faith. If it's Luke you want, then I'll get him for you. I have his telephone number somewhere.' He squeezed her hand, and gave her a long look from beneath his bushy eyebrows. 'I wish you well, Faith Charteris,' he said, 'and I will say this,' he went on as his dark eyes filled with a tranquil mockery, 'you very nearly led me astray.'

Faith's voice shook with emotion. 'Don't say that, Sebastian. I'll never think of you like that.'

'You will think of me, then?' He drew her a little closer.

'Of course!' She stared helplessly into his eyes. 'You know I will.'

'I'm glad.' With narrowed eyes he searched her face. 'But you're still determined to leave us as quickly as you can?'

'I must,' she said, drawing away from him. 'And I would like to get in touch with Luke this morning,' she lied. Even her lie seemed to have an undertone of innocence. 'I'm supposed to be staying with his parents. Luke knew that I'd get in touch with him as soon as I'd seen you.'

'I see. Very well.' Sebastian spoke in a tired voice now, and Faith's heart broke as she watched him get up and move heavily across the room back to the door. She wanted to shout after him, 'You have a wife, Sebastian! You can't deceive her!'

Leave me my dignity, she thought as she desperately covered her face with her hands the moment the door closed sharply after him. For a while she stood trembling with emotion, unsure again, undecided, even wavering.

Then Gloria came into the room and told her that Luke Webb was waiting to speak to her on the telephone. Faith whispered, 'Thank you,' and sped to the phone as quickly as she could. Downstairs in the small, cosy sitting room she pantingly picked up the receiver. 'Hello!' she gasped. 'Luke?'

'Hello, baby! What the devil are you up to now?'

Faith thought she would burst into tears. 'Luke,' she faltered, 'where are you?'

'In the big city, of course. The old man knew where to find me.'

'I thought you'd gone home?'

'Not yet. Plenty of time for that.' Luke's laugh was significant.

'I'd like to go with you, Luke.'

'What!' Luke's voice burst through the receiver. 'I thought you were living it up with the old man. Dancing round the village green and all that jazz.'

'Don't be silly, Luke.' There was a sharp edge to Faith's voice now.

'Well, I suppose not. But don't tell me he's got you a nursing job. I know all about his sister Gloria. She's a bit of an invalid, isn't she? I know he's always worrying about her. Doesn't like leaving her, apparently.'

His sister! His sister! Luke's words rose like a great suffocating wave in Faith's confused brain. She began to sway. 'Luke,' she gasped. 'I'll ring you again. And I love you, I really do ...'

'What the devil—!'

Faith dropped the receiver on Luke's exclamation, then she stood like a marble statue, and her face just as white. Joy, dismay, everything she felt for Sebastian welled up in her and for a moment she thought she would pass out with sheer joy. Gloria was Sebastian's sister! But why hadn't she guessed? Why was she so distrustful? Why had she again doubted Sebastian's integrity? Shuddering, sobbing a little with relief, she flopped weakly down on to the nearest chair. She could not believe it! But Luke had told her so, and Luke knew everything about Sebastian.

At last Faith stood up again and breathlessly she went to find Gloria. She found her in a large kitchen busy filling a vase with roses. 'Gloria,' she whispered, and went up to her and put her arm about her waist. 'Gloria, I must speak to you. I've made a terrible mistake. In fact I don't know how to tell you, but I thought you were Sebastian's wife.' With a sob she confessed, 'Of course I don't want to leave Mill House—or either of you, for that matter. I don't know what to say.'

Gloria Hillard's lovely throat worked as she stared back at the slight girl who stood with her head bowed before her. Then she gently steered her towards the door of the conservatory. 'My dear,' she said gently, 'you've no idea how pleased I am. I just couldn't work this one out. Now I understand, and I think I have myself to blame. I didn't introduce myself, did I—but then I was so ill.' She gave Faith another encouraging little push. 'We'll talk later,' she said encouragingly as they reached another door. 'You'll think of what to say, Faith, but you must say it to Sebastian. He's out there in the garden.'

The garden at the back of Mill House was large, walled and sheltered by a copse of tall pine trees. It was full of soft sounds and sweet smells and the sky above it was a brilliant blue streaked only by a few goat-hair clouds. Faith saw Sebastian and she went straight to his side, telling him in a little choking voice, 'Sebastian, I love you. I want you to forgive me. I actually thought Gloria was your wife—that was why I was running away again.'

She watched him straighten up and heard his quick intake of breath, but he said nothing as his arm tightened about her and for a while they both just stood staring at the sunlight as it moved across the gray wall. Then, slowly, they turned and gazed into each other's eyes. Helplessly, Faith listened to the mad drumming of her heart, then she whispered, 'Kiss me, Sebastian. Kiss me again and tell me that I'm forgiven.'

Gently he kissed her, a long sweet kiss. Then, still silently, he put his arm about her and steered her back into the house and into the small back room, where he took her in his arms again. He kissed her again and again. Slowly his lips slid down her straight nose, to her lips now parted and offered eagerly to him, then down to the long fluid line of her young throat. With a muffled groan of rapture he swept her up into his arms and carried her to the velvet-covered sofa by the window and gently eased her down on to it. She stared up at him as though spellbound. She raised her arms to his neck, drew him down, down. Tenderly she scanned his dark, magnificent face, and then it seemed to her that nothing existed any longer but their lips, their hard, eager bodies and the sound of Sebastian's deep murmurings of love against her hair.

'You do love me?' she whispered, and now a trace of anxiety tinged her voice. 'You do?'

'I do,' Sebastian said in a tone of sombre finality and as his kisses grew more passionate: 'Oh, Faith! How can I tell you how I despaired at the thought of being without you? At the idea of you going back to Webb.' He drew away from her now, and stood up as though giving time for his passion to cool a little. He laughed a little, 'You know, your journey up here wasn't really necessary. I've given up the sea, Faith. I'm going into business. I have an engineering concern which I now intend to look after myself. I never intended to go back to the *English Rose*.'

'I see.' Faith looked at him playfully. 'So I can go?'

'Never!' His eyes burned down into hers now. His dark throat worked and his strong body grew taut as he straightened up. 'Never!' he said again, and this time his voice rang with the passion he strove to control. 'You'll never leave me again, Faith—I'll make sure of that.' His eyes grew soft as he sat down again on the edge of the sofa and drawing her hand into his own, he told her with some of the old authority which thrilled her so much, 'You're going to marry me, of course,' and as he studied her still, sweet face, 'and cause me a lot of trouble, I suppose . . .'

Faith nestled against him. 'Oh, Sebastian,' she whispered, 'I'll never cause you any trouble again.' She looked deep into his eyes. 'If I do, then you can lock me up again,' she told him breathlessly. 'You can do anything you like with me, Sebastian, because I love you so much. I trust you so much!'

'Then the first thing I must do is marry you,' Sebastian said, and pursed his lips mischievously. 'Preferably, of course, when you don't happen to have a black eye.'

Faith laughed and drew close to him again as he tenderly traced the lobe of her ear with his lips, flooding her whole being with delicious sensation. 'You're so wonderful, Sebastian,' she whispered. 'So wonderful!'

He stood up again, but this time his face was grave, his eyes full of a profound tenderness, as he stared down at her. His voice was warm and controlled as he took her hand and said, 'Come, my love, let's tell Gloria the good news.'

Harlequin Presents...

By popular demand...
24 original novels from this series—by 7 of the world's greatest romance authors.

These back issues have been out of print for some time. So don't miss out; order your copies now!

Harlequin Reader Service
ORDER FORM

Mail coupon to:
Harlequin Reader Service
M.P.O. Box 707
Niagara Falls, New York 14302

Canadian Residents send to:
649 Ontario St.
Stratford, Ont. N5A 6W2

Please send me by return mail the Harlequin Presents that I have checked.
I am enclosing $1.25 for each book ordered.

Please check volumes requested:

☐ 38	☐ 46	☐ 54
☐ 39	☐ 47	☐ 55
☐ 40	☐ 48	☐ 56
☐ 41	☐ 49	☐ 57
☐ 42	☐ 50	☐ 58
☐ 43	☐ 51	☐ 59
☐ 44	☐ 52	☐ 60
☐ 45	☐ 53	☐ 61

Number of books ordered_____ @ $1.25 each = $ _____

N.Y. and N.J. residents add appropriate sales tax $ _____

Postage and handling = $ _____ .25

TOTAL = $ _____

NAME _____
(please print)

ADDRESS _____

CITY _____

STATE/PROV. _____ ZIP/POSTAL CODE _____

ROM 2157